Talkin'

Squirrel

Blues

Pádraig Hanratty

For the koala

Also available:

A Blanket of Blues

Everybody gets the blues sometimes. Fingers Flaherty had them all the time. He lived the blues and sang about his every ache.

Flaherty's blues gave him nothing but hardship, sore feet and a shattered heart. Every one of his songs told a fraught story. His characters walked many a dark path and twisted lane on their troubled journeys.

And now they get to share their tales, wrapped in dark humour and a blanket of blues.

A collection of short stories inspired by Flaherty's songs, A BLANKET OF BLUES presents its varied cast at turning points in their lives. Some yearn for change, whereas others seek self-improvement. And others want nothing more than a little peace of mind, even for just a few hours. Each character struggles through the daily conflicts and irritations of his or her life, fighting back with proud confidence, caustic wit, mule-headed defiance and a dash of reckless optimism.

Dimestore Avenue Blues

Jesse believes that the future will be better. One day, he'll make up for all his mistakes and achieve perfection.

He still has some bad days as he lives out his autumn years in Dublin. But his worst days were in New York in 1976. After that city had nearly crushed him, he'd fled to Dublin, a broken man. But he was determined to rebuild himself, brick by brick, improving day by day.

Back in the 1970s, Jesse was a successful young ad man on Madison Avenue. He'd succeeded because he was willing, indeed eager, to do anything to advance his career. It all seemed like a good plan, right up until the day he brought a pistol to work. For years in those offices and meeting rooms, they all thought they were kings, living it up in their high palaces of power. As it all fell apart for Jesse in 1976, he realised they were all just fumbling in the dimestore.

Jesse knows he isn't perfect. He's made many mistakes and will probably make more in the future. Now, with the possibility of contentment finally within his grasp, will he be allowed one final chance to be happy? Or will the ghosts from his past once again refuse to lie down in their graves?

Prologue

Teddy Bear Bites Moses... Bear Unhurt

She's chopping my vegetables, she's cooking my meat.
I can't even stand on my own three feet.
I've burnt my fingers on her body heat!
Protect me from the Edgy Woman Blues.

Edgy Woman Blues
Fingers Flaherty

"You're not even listening to me, Moses!" Natalie threw the small Oxford souvenir teddy bear at the inert figure on the sofa. "I'd get more attention from this bear."

"Hmmmm?" Moses McNamara was not one of life's great multi-taskers. In fact, a single task was often beyond his abilities. For now, his attention was more or less riveted to the newspaper obituary he was reading. Nothing, not even a flying teddy bear flung by a fraught girlfriend, would distract him. However, he realised that he was still expected to make some token contribution to the conversation. "Um... sure... eh?"

Fingers Flaherty
Singer, songwriter, outlaw
1938–2012

Fingers Flaherty's drunken death last night in a car crash will come as a shock to his few fans. And yet, for him to die inebriated behind the wheel of a smashed Ford was disappointingly predictable. A predictable shock. Flaherty's death, like everything else about him, is a contradiction. As he said in his 1963 debut album, *Fingers on the Blues*: "Ashes to ashes, sand to sand/Both sides of the coin in my own hand."

Flaherty's life was a contradiction of his own making. When I last interviewed him, he still claimed to be devoted to his integrity. We both knew he would do anything for a few more seconds of fame. In his constant quest for commercial success, he tried on one ludicrous mask after another. He completely lost his way in the process. "I'm not always sure which part of me is hiding," he said in a 1986 interview. "I can't remember if this is the real me or if I'm in disguise."

"What the hell am I doing here?" Natalie sadly shook her head and then gathered her energy for the full verbal assault. "You've changed, Moses. I hardly recognise you anymore. We're in the land where teardrops fall now. It used to be so much fun. Jesus, the last time we had a really good laugh together was at Wino Wally's funeral! Six months ago! You're nothing more than a moody, selfish twenty-five-year-old adolescent. With all the personality of sour –"

"Can't you turn down the volume?" Moses just about managed to switch from one task to the other. "I'm trying to read the bastarding paper."

"You care more about Fingers bastarding Flaherty than you do about me!"

Although Moses wouldn't admit it, Natalie was right. This time, anyway. The death of Fingers Flaherty, his shabby idol, pushed all other matters out of his field of vision.

In all his years as a blues singer, Fingers never got to eat the commercial cake. He'd nibbled it once in 1964 when his comic ballad "Backseat Blues" became a minor hit. It was a love song, of sorts: "I don't want to be cured, sugar, I won't swallow your pill/If your sweet love don't kill me, sugar, then your bitter hatred will."

His *Mississippi Money Blues* album had sold well on the back of that single. He seemed to find a welcoming audience among the acid-stoned university students of the time. "None of this is real to me," he once told *The Irish Chord*. "I feel like I'm making the whole bloody thing up as I go along. Every song tells a story. And none of the stories are true. Are they?"

"Tony from Accounts is always giving me the eye." Natalie decided to attack from another angle. "And he's real fit too. At least *he* notices me! To think I've been giving him the brush-off because of you. I look back and wonder if I've been tripping this last two years."

"Why is there a teddy bear on my lap?"

"The bear gets more attention than I do!"

"Sure. Whatever."

For the most of the 1960s, Fingers was a respected blues singer. In his songs, he told of his quest for the ideal woman. His career, however, was a quest for an audience. He ploughed a solitary furrow and managed to appeal to just enough people to be able to stay on the road.

In the 1970s, his tiny audience outgrew him. Fingers desperately tried to appeal to the market, any market. "I'm yours for a dollar, babe," he begged in "Hollow Whorehouse Blues".

"All the girls at work tell me I'd get a better catch for a few euros down at the pet shop. Or the graveyard."

"Suppose so… Any chance of you staying quiet until I've read this article?"

"If you're not going on about that dead blues singer, you're whinging about this performance appraisal you have coming up next month. You need help, Moses."

"I need help getting some peace and quiet."

In the mid-1980s, Fingers had a tiny renaissance. Ballybaboon Butter used one of his songs, "Spread Your Love On Me", in an advertising campaign. His battered voice croaked across the national airwaves every evening for about two months.

His record company desperately patched together a compilation album in an attempt to rekindle interest. Maybe fifty people got interested. Fingers disappeared as suddenly as he had reappeared. His comeback album, *A Blanket of Blues*, failed to rekindle enough interest. He continued to play tiny halls and pubs all over the country, but fewer and fewer people seemed to care. At one show, he got into a fight with members of the audience and ended up in hospital.

"Look, Moses, I think it's best if we take a break for a while, before we kill each other. I think we just need to get off this train and see where exactly we are."

"What are you looking for a train for? You going somewhere?"

"I don't know where I'm going with you anymore."

"I think there's a timetable in that drawer over there. Hidden in with all the other shit I dump in there."

"Goodbye, Moses!"

Last night, Fingers drove his battered Ford into a street lamp. He had just finished a gig in Cork and celebrated by polishing off a bottle of whiskey.

Earlier that evening, he sang his "Bloodshot Blues": "There's a strange thin man knock knockin' at my door/Pass me that bottle quick, I don't wanna be sober no more."

For once, it seemed that he could see exactly where the tracks were leading.

Moses glanced up when he heard the front door slam.

He looked down at the Oxford teddy bear.

"Do you know where she's gone to?"

Moses tried to put Natalie out of his mind as he sat down for his performance review.

His light-brown hair was styled into an executive cut and his clean-shaven face radiated inner energy. He wore a blue "power suit", stretched by taut muscles. The office sparkled in the reflection of his polished shoes.

Moses's voice rang out as he explained his achievements to his boss, Coconut Fred. He'd never sounded so confident in his life. This was a winner's voice. A voice that trampled over self-doubt and threw indecision in the ditch.

Coconut Fred listened to that voice, rapt. At thirty-nine, Fred had played the corporate game for fifteen years. By now, he'd become jaded by the office dramas and pointless politics. Today, however, he nodded in eager agreement with Moses, smiling at the clever witticisms.

When Moses stopped talking, Fred cleared his throat.

"That's very impressive, Moses… Gosh, I'm almost lost for words. Ha ha ha."

"I try my best, Mr Hearty," Moses said with a corporate smile. "Though I am sure that I can do even better."

"Yes, I'm sure you can continue to impress us. The spark that has got me this far, I can see it in you too. If we had more people like you, this company could march through any recession and still blow away the stock market's expectations. Now, if you don't mind, there are just a few questions I'd like to ask you. Let's start with this one, then." Fred picked up a card from his desk and smiled. "What can you tell me about the economic policies of King Richard II?"

Moses stared at Fred.

King Richard II? What the hell has he got to do with anything?

But Moses suddenly remembered that King Richard II was a vital part of the review. He'd simply forgotten to do his homework. His heart began beating frantically as he realised that it was now too late. Beads of warm sweat trickled down the back of his neck.

"I… well… I think it's… em… like, you know… I don't know… I'm sorry."

Fred's face darkened dramatically. Without warning, he threw a coconut at Moses.

Moses yelped as the coconut smashed into his stomach.

"We'll try another question before I decide whether to fire you." Fred's voice quivered with menace. "Identify some of the distinctive cinematic devices used in early Elvis Presley films."

"I'm sorry, Mr Hearty." All the self-confidence had evaporated out of Moses's voice. He could almost see the steam escaping from his mouth. "I… I…"

Panic surged through him, making his chest heave in raw gasps.

His armpits were soaking. His neat haircut uncombed itself into a dishevelled bird's nest.

"Are you stupid, you pathetic little prick?" Fred roared, flinging another coconut at him. "I devour useless bastards like you for breakfast!"

The coconut struck Moses on the forehead. Blinding pain erupted inside his head. The room spun around violently.

"Here's an easy one for you! Explain why Natalie left you, McNamara."

Moses's clothes began to disintegrate. When he tried to speak, he bit his tongue. He looked up at Fred in shivering despair, blood drooling down his chin.

"Don't you know anything?" Fred launched another coconut. "Why did she leave you?"

"What are you talking about?" Moses began weeping as the coconut struck his knee. "She only went out to get the papers."

The last of his clothes collapsed to the floor in a puff of blue dust. He shivered there, naked, clutching his stinging knee. Shattered bone crumbled beneath the flesh. He looked up at Fred, through blood-soaked eyes.

Oh shit!

Fred had changed.

Completely.

Fred had turned into a large teddy bear. A savage teddy bear in a brown suit. The stench of the teddy bear's breath hit Moses like a wet towel.

The teddy bear clenched a coconut in its hand.

"Please," Moses begged, "I'll tweet the best marketing copy in history."

The teddy bear flung the coconut.

Moses woke up with a bolt. The bedside clock said 4.15 am. It took him ten minutes to calm down after the nightmare. Eventually, he slipped back to shivering sleep.

And then he dreamt about Natalie… again.

The clock is striking thirteen, she must be back in town,
Wearing her razor-blade stockings and barb-wire gown,
Stabbing the teddy bear, cuddling the clown.
Protect me from the Edgy Woman Blues.

Edgy Woman Blues
Fingers Flaherty

Always On My Mind

Anonymous Blues

Maybe I didn't treat you like a warrior queen,
You know it's true, I probably didn't treat you like a warrior queen.
My hose was way too dry, Lord, to turn her garden green.
There ain't no name for these blues.

Take that woman off my mind, Lord, kick her out of my head.
Take her off my mind, dear Lord, kick that woman out of my head.
She's drinkin' from a different cup, sleepin' in a lanky stranger's bed.
There ain't no name for these blues.

Blues jumpin' out of the bush, blues crawlin' on the floor,
Blue's drippin' down the walls, blues knockin' on the door,
Blues scratchin' at my leg, blues ringin' in my ear,
Blues smokin' my cigarette, blues drinkin' up my beer.

Santa's crawlin' up her chimney, Lord, monkey man at her back door,
Santa's in that chimney, Lord, the monkey man's out that back door.
I'll be your salty dog, baby, sleepin' on a pallet on your floor.
There ain't no name for these blues.

The judge cleared his throat, he said he didn't want to condemn me.
The judge, he cleared his throat, sayin' he didn't want to condemn me.
The blues sat on the jury, Lord, sayin' they could never set me free.
There ain't no name for these blues.

Chapter 1

Going Forward To The Promised Land

The sun shone on the silver water.
My wife just left me for the fisherman's daughter.
I look up in disbelief,
Nothing I say will bring relief.
God gave us famine, God gave us slaughter,
God gave me the curse of the fisherman's daughter.

Blues From A Fisherman's Daughter
Fingers Flaherty

"I saw a squirrel walking into work today," Moses said, shuddering as the coffee slithered down his throat and sizzled its way to his stomach. "Imagine that!"

The coffee blend this morning was a frisky mix of Java beans, kerosene and sulphuric acid. In the latest round of panic-stricken budget cuts, Aztech Software had changed its coffee supplier. Rumours persisted that the new coffee was smuggled out by moonlight from underground laboratories in Iran.

Apart from Coconut Fred, the entire Marketing division were at the breakfast table in the Aztech canteen. In the harsh morning sunlight, the canteen always looked like it had been designed by some spiteful feng shui consultant on acid. In reality, it was designed by Gobsmack Design, Dublin's most "cost-effective" (in other words "cheapest") interior space consultancy service. Gobsmack was run by

Xavier, the Aztech finance director's brother. Unfortunately, the morning Gobsmack started the contract, Xavier's wife ran away with Sister Amy from the local convent. Xavier was understandably distraught by the unexpected result of his wife's dabbling in spiritual yoga. The Aztech canteen became a visible manifestation of his inner turmoil.

The dark blue plastic tables were chaotically scattered around the red and green floor tiles. The sinister 3D abstract graphics and etchings that dotted the grey walls dared employees to interpret them. Instead of inducing a warm inner calm, the canteen décor conspired with the food to induce a constant sense of sea-sickness.

The Marketing division looked particularly sea-sick this morning. Lydia Maguire, twenty-eight years old in a navy-blue blouse and black skirt, delicately buttered her toast, frowning at the tiny crumbs that collapsed on to the tangerine table.

Beside her, Roger Flanaghan, his razor-sharp bottle-green suit glistening in the sunlight, munched his breakfast cereal. He was thirty, with receding ginger hair, and was an expert corporate player.

Paul Ryan, the twenty-three-year-old new boy in the office, reluctantly sipped his orange juice, his hands trembling. His cream suit looked like it had been slept in and his unshaven face looked like it had been hanging on a clothesline all night.

Sandra White was drinking a cup of coffee. Her eyes darted around the canteen, trying to pick up any careless crumbs of gossip. She was thirty-four and had worked for Aztech for seven years. Her loyalty to the company amounted to a grudging acknowledgement that the wages helped to pay for the 100%-financed mortgage on her 100%-

overpriced tiny apartment in the city centre.

"I said, I saw a squirrel walking into work today," Moses reminded everyone. "Does nobody care about anything I say?"

"Listen to Moses." Lydia sniggered. "The coffee must have corroded his brain. He saw a squirrel walking into work! I thought you studied English at college, Moses. Don't you know where to place your modifiers?"

"I know where I'd like to shove them!" Moses was in no mood for work today, let alone listening to Lydia's jibes. "What's your point?"

"You saw a squirrel *when you were* walking into work. The squirrel wasn't walking into work, was he? Was he wearing a little suit? Or is it dress-down day in his company?"

"Or maybe," broke in Roger, laughing his formal laugh, "he was on his way to college to learn how to construct his sentences correctly."

Lydia and Sandra started laughing. Paul was still too shattered to muster up a smile. His face settled instead into a death's head grimace.

Moses sulked in silence, hoping his colleagues would be mugged by baseball-bat-wielding squirrels on the way home.

To cheer himself up, he recalled his singular encounter with the squirrel…

It had been on Cartright Road around 8.00 that morning as Moses made his reluctant way to work. Turning the corner into Cartright Road always felt like turning the corner into another world. It was Dublin's suburbia at its most paranoid. The lawns were always perfectly presentable and the residents' minor misdemeanours and intriguing little fetishes were always perfectly hidden behind exquisitely curtained windows. The very air seemed to crackle with nervous tension. The leaves fluttered timidly, afraid to disturb the quiet. Locals called it Mahogany Row.

Moses stood alone on the road. All was as silent as a Zen vacuum.

Suddenly, something rustled in one of the hedges.

A small furry creature jumped out in front of Moses.

A squirrel! On Cartright Road! Good God, who'd ever think you'd meet a squirrel here? I thought they executed rodents by lethal injection on this road.

The squirrel stared at Moses.

Moses stared back.

For a few fuzzy seconds, Moses thought that the squirrel was actually smiling at him. A furry, benevolent smile. Telling him to lighten up, that life is not so bad after all, that today might end up being one of the best days of his life. Its eyes glowed with inner warmth.

The squirrel started looking around and then, as if suddenly remembering some important date, scurried down the road, its tail swishing playfully after it.

Moses gazed after the squirrel. It was the friendliest, most lovable little creature he'd ever seen. He hadn't been so attracted to a fellow creature since that afternoon long ago when he'd first seen Natalie jogging in the park. He could imagine taming the squirrel, taking it home as a pet. Giving it a goofy name. Like Ernie. He pictured himself talking to it in the evening, telling it all his problems.

We'd have a blast together!

"And you should have seen the wine they were serving," Lydia was now moaning. "It was so –"

"Oh, shut up about your stupid bloody dinner party, Lydia,"

snapped Sandra. "The only dinner parties we'll be going to are down in the soup kitchen! Is there nothing more interesting to talk about? Like why Paul looks like a torn sack of shit this morning. Our balance sheet looks healthier than he does."

"Leave me alone." Paul noisily rubbed his ashen face. "I didn't get home until 5.00 this morning. We were at a reunion of the college class in Sexy Sadie's on London Street. I don't know if I'm coming out of a hangover or falling into one. One minute I was dancing with this hot little yoke in the moonlight and drinking some cocktail that's on fire, the next I was waking up in bed on another planet at 8.00 this morning. Jesus Christ, I think I'm still drunk."

"It looks like he was burning the candle at both ends last night," said Roger.

"He looks like he was burning his face at both ends," Sandra replied.

"Leave him alone, Sandra," said Moses, pushing his caustic coffee cup away from him. "He can do without you poking your two cents into his eye. It's not as if you've never come in hungover. Remember that hen night you were at last week? You came into work the next day looking like you'd slept in an electric chair."

"Oooh, someone's in a twitchy mood today." Sandra laughed. "Easy knowing you're shitting a bucket of bricks about your performance review. You'll be playing the mangled martyr all day."

Moses had his annual performance review with Frederick Hearty in the afternoon. He had filled out his review form last night, rehearsing his lines until they began to lose all meaning.

"I'll be fine." Moses didn't convince even himself. "No bother."

I asked for coffee, she gave me water.
She's dancin' in the moonlight with the fisherman's daughter.
I'm gonna get drunk on turpentine,
Petrol, bleach and rosé wine.
She's in there chewin' with the teeth I bought her,
I hope she bites the hand off the fisherman's daughter.

Blues From A Fisherman's Daughter
Fingers Flaherty

Moses sat in his mauve cubicle, listening to his Fingers Flaherty mp3s. Flaherty was roaring about a fisherman's daughter. Listening to personal mp3s was, of course, strictly against company policy so Moses, of course, ignored this policy and listened to as many mp3s as possible before going home. These tiny, insignificant acts of rebellion helped get him through the day. Unfortunately, his audio player's tendency to crash after every third song dampened his rebellious fervour.

On Moses's computer, the Oxford teddy bear sat contentedly. As usual, it was having a more productive day than Moses was.

An e-mail arrived from Coconut Fred.

Moses, I need an eight-point bulleted list explaining why DA13 is suitable for college students. Say something about how we're trending towards helping them leverage their studies. Action ASAP. Frederick

Moses aimlessly gazed at the e-mail for some minutes.

Everything's a bloody bulleted list with him. His autobiography would

probably be just a series of list items.

Over in cubicle 7A, Paul was phoning friends, trying to piece together what happened in Sexy Sadie's last night.

"Well, what did she look like? … Only sixteen? … Jesus Christ! Did anything happen? … How did I screw it up? … No way! I'd never call anyone a corpo slut. … Oh, I see. … No, I don't suppose I'd normally call you a lousy, deceitful, two-faced wanker. Sorry, man. I was drunk. Well, I suppose you know that. … I actually feel like I've been poisoned. …"

Moses started typing.

Domestic Accountant 2013 will help you fail your exams more spectacularly than ever because it will

- give you muscle pains where you never thought you had muscles
- make you go blind (and deaf, if you are using the audio-compliant version)
- drive you to crack cocaine
- destroy what miserable little sex life you have

Moses deleted the document. It was a bad day to test Coconut Fred's sense of humour.

Oh well, must look on the bright side. When you get an e-mail from Fred, you always know it's going to be the worst e-mail of the day.

He turned off the audio player and spun gently around in his swivel chair, deciding it really was time that he started pretending to be busy.

However, before starting on his project, he clicked on a news website to see whether anyone else in the world was having a thoroughly miserable day already. The one-minute news video would enlighten him and put his own wretchedness into perspective.

It was then Moses noticed that a new e-mail had come in.

This one was from Natalie.

"And now," the newscaster was saying, "the latest financial news."

Moses took a deep breath and opened the e-mail.

Hello Moses,

I really hope you are keeping well! Things have started to pick up with me. I'm beginning to get my life back together.

"And the euro is down slightly against the dollar but, as you can see, up somewhat against the yen…"

Sorry I haven't been in touch much this last month. But anyway, the time has come to bury the past. I think that we've both got over all that shit that hit the fan a few weeks ago. I realise that the day after Fingers Flaherty died wasn't really the best time for me to call it a day, but that's the past now.

Time to move on. Time to get going.

"In other news, the Italian Prime Minister finds himself waking up to another political scandal this morning following the discovery of an ostrich in his…"

Bear with me. This is a tough e-mail for me. But sometimes I find it easier to put the words into an e-mail than try to explain my thoughts to you in person. You know I always prefer to think before I let the words loose. Unlike you!

I suppose what I am trying to say is "Goodbye". I don't think we ever said that to each other in the end. We said enough other stuff, but never that. Well, maybe I did, but I'm sure you weren't listening.

I know that this comes as no shock. I mean, we've both moved on from that place. But I think we need to bury the ghosts. I don't want to be haunted forever.

"Prince Philip has said that his controversial remarks about hairdressers were taken completely out of context..."

I got promoted to team leader on the Red Wolf project at work. You know how long I've been trying for that! I didn't think they'd promote anyone because the company is still licking its wounds after the disastrous e-cookery initiative. Talk about biting off more than we could chew!

"Two missing pandas have been found safe and well in a butcher's shop in Brighton..."

I've sort of started kind of going out with this guy at work. You may remember him. Tony Lyons? The guy in Accounts. You said he looked like he'd been used as a rope in a tug of war contest. It's nothing serious. Yet. We're just having a laugh together. It's good to remember what that feels like. Have you found someone special yet?

Anyway, I hope you are keeping well. Like me, you've been backwards through the blender. But I'm sure you've managed to piece yourself back together. You were never a Humpty Dumpty.

Let's move on. Take good care of yourself.

Natalie

Moses had enough to worry about with his review later in the afternoon. He was determined not to think about Natalie.

Don't start thinking about all that shit today. Time to empty my mind.

Meditate on the sound of one paw clapping.

Moses found himself thinking about Natalie. His surroundings faded into a blur of white computers, mauve cubicle walls and chipped grey ceiling tiles. The noise of the printers was a hypnotic fuzz.

All that was in focus was Natalie's face.

Pale skin. Faint freckles. Ginger hair. Dark coffee eyes. Smiling a smile that could drag the sun out of the darkest, sulkiest cloud.

What harm can a quick phone call do?

Moses took his phone out of his pocket and scrolled to her number. He'd probably get round to deleting the number some day. But not today.

"Hi, Natalie," he said when she answered. "It's Moses."

"Moses?" She sounded disappointed. Then wary. "What… do you want?"

"Er… I just read your e-mail."

"Oh! I see… Well…"

"I… em… just wanted to congratulate you on the promotion." Moses began to suspect that the phone call was a mistake. "Fair play!"

"Thanks." She sounded like she was searching under her desk for a hole that would willingly swallow her up. "So if that's –"

"That's all I wanted to say. Thanks for… you know… letting me know and all."

"That's fine… How are things with you?"

"Great! Super! Maybe we could meet up for a drink? To celebrate your promotion?"

"I don't know, Moses. It might –"

"Just a drink. Nothing else. You know, just to…" Moses's voice trailed off hopelessly. "Whatever."

"I don't think it's such a good idea."

"Oh…" *Be like that!* "Okay."

"It's best that we stay out of each other's way for a while, Moses. Like, this thing with Tony is still in the early stages –"

"How is Tony anyway?" *I bet the big, long, lanky, bandy-legged, ugly rake of a thing's useless in the sack!* "Is he… treating you well? Can he even get it –?"

"Goodbye, Moses."

Moses listened to the dead hum of the phone as the teddy bear stared at him accusingly.

Has she found out what Tony is like in the sack? Has she even… Oh, fuck this! I need to get away from the desk for a while.

He got up and walked to the office bathroom.

He splashed cold water on his face and blindly reached out to grab a paper towel. Drying his face, he assessed his reflection in the mirror.

"Although I say it myself, Fred, I believe that I have been an outstanding employee. I have successfully achieved all my allocated vague pointless deliverables in a schedule-compatible manner that enhanced our economic engagement with the market turmoil. I am a leveraged human capital resource utilising my personal energy cycle… so don't start throwing coconuts at me, you bastard!"

Moses wasn't entirely happy with his reflection. Although of average height and slim build, his slumped gallows-bound posture made him look insignificant. He stretched himself into a more erect, imposing stance.

That's better… Slightly… Try not to look so condemned…

His hair was tidily parted. He had shaved carefully this morning, but his face still didn't look refreshed. His mouth drooped slightly. A veil of tiredness hung around the eyes. Even his ears seemed to hang listlessly.

Jesus, I look like I haven't slept in weeks! That squirrel had more zest for life than I do.

Just over two years ago, Moses started working for Aztech Software, in the Marketing division. The job involved writing marketing literature he didn't believe in for software packages that he didn't fully understand. His current projects included DataBasics XI, Domestic Accountant 13 and Scribbler Prof. Before joining Aztech, Moses had written a thesis about existential dilemmas in Shakespeare. His college supervisor, a Chartreuse-soaked martyr to perpetual toothaches and sexual harassment claims, told him that it was the most "original, unusual" thesis he'd ever read. Even when he graduated, Moses wasn't sure whether this was a compliment.

"Let's talk about these software packages, Fred… I have personal experience of Domestic Accountant. I have interfaced with it in real time. It is the most useless, pathetic little spiteful bastard of a program ever created. And now that the whole economy has collapsed, no one will buy the fucker! People don't need a stupid computer package to tell them they're broke."

Natalie had taught Moses many things. She taught him that he wasn't the centre of the entire universe. Indeed, she often reminded him that he wasn't even the centre of *her* universe. She taught him how to apologise graciously. She taught him how to cook a curry without reducing the kitchen to a charred shell. She taught him how to use the new DVD player.

Moses thought that the most useless thing she taught him was creative visualisation. Natalie was an enthusiastic believer in positive thinking; she once remarked that she had to be, given whom she was going out with. For her, yoga and meditation were precious opportunities to briefly retreat from the chaotic currents of life and relax on the blissful shore. She tried to teach Moses how to meditate, but his chronic inability to stay awake during the sessions led to the whole enterprise being abandoned.

Instead, she tried to show him the benefits of creative visualisation, a process of creating a detailed mental image of your goal in order to motivate yourself to achieve it. One night, she became suspicious when Moses refused to tell her what he was visualising. Moses was impressed at how detailed he could make his fantasies, even when it became obvious that Natalie wouldn't be helping to achieve that particular goal that night.

Figuring he had nothing to lose, Moses decided to give creative visualisation another go. He pictured himself giving the performance report of his life. He pictured Coconut Fred's jaw bouncing on the floor in awestruck admiration. He pictured a squirrel smiling at him, friendly encouragement twinkling in his eyes.

Get a clear picture of it in your head. Picture that bastard's face. Picture him wetting himself in his admiration. Picture him raiding the pension fund in order to give you a raise. Picture him –

Paul stumbled into the bathroom, his hand to his mouth.

"Hi, Paul! Feeling any better?"

Without even trying to answer, Paul ran over to the sink beside

Moses. He closed his eyes tightly and gripped the sides of the basin.

And braced himself.

Then he vomited into the sink. Still-warm coffee and spit and chewed bread gushed from his mouth. His face turned skeleton pale. Tiny beads of sweat broke out on his forehead as the first wave subsided.

"Jesus Christ, Paul! Did you have to do that?"

"Yes." Paul let out an agonised groan. "I did."

"I've got my review this afternoon and the last thing I need to see is you puking your ring up in front of me. I saw enough of that at the office party."

Paul gingerly splashed warm water on himself. After some seconds, the blood crawled back to his face.

Moses turned his attention to his reflection. He needed more creative visualisation. He tried to picture Coconut Fred nodding his head, telling him what a fantastic job he'd done.

However, all he could picture was Paul walking into the review at a crucial moment, just when Moses was about to deliver his killer punchline.

All he could picture was Paul walking up behind Coconut Fred and vomiting all over him.

My wife cast her net and she caught her,
Fell hook, line and sinker for the fisherman's daughter.
I'll phone her up and ask her what she's doing with my wife,
I'll phone her up and ask her why she wanted to ruin my life.
Time to get up and take a walk down by the water,

And see if it will drown the fisherman's daughter.

Blues From A Fisherman's Daughter
Fingers Flaherty

At 2.00 that afternoon, Moses knocked tentatively on the open door of Fred Hearty's office.

Go down, Moses, way down in Egypt land. Tell ol' pharaoh let my human resources go.

Fred looked up from his pathologically tidy desk.

"Come in, Moses."

Fred seemed to be in a good mood. He was in casual dress, with black slacks and a short-sleeved blue shirt, open at the neck. His black hair was slightly dishevelled and he appeared to be making a genuine effort to suppress his instinctive contempt for Moses.

Sitting down, Moses noticed that Fred's open collar exposed some of the hairs on his chest. He also noticed that Fred's arms were quite hairy. Apart from that, Fred did not really look like a teddy bear.

"Well, Moses," Fred said, indulging in a carefully practiced smile, "you know the drill, as the dentist said to the bishop. I just want to remind you that you are not on trial here. I'm no judge or anything. No one is going to be fired... today. This is to be an open exchange of views, a co-operative attempt to map out your career path in the current challenging climate. We are going to recognise your achievements over the last twelve difficult months and identify opportunities for improvement going forward within the necessary confines of our cost-containment initiatives. We'll table ideas and run them up the flagpole. Is that all clear?"

"Yes, Fred. It's crystal clear. In fact, I think —"

"This year is a key year for us. Going forward, we will be transitioning into an aggressive sales strategy in order to incentivise the materialisation of our vision. Our sales have had a disconnect with expectations this last few months, but you sometimes have to go through the desert in order to reach the Promised Land. We must put our ducks in a row and manage their expectations. But, needless to say, they're not fish in a barrel."

"Of course not." *What the fuck is he talking about?* "It has been… a challenge."

"We don't have to cover everything today. We can take some of the issues offline and park them on the sidebar. For now, let's concentrate on organic growth. So tell me what you think you have achieved over the last year." Fred leaned back in the chair and folded his arms. "Identify some key actioned deliverables."

Feeling like he was about to deliver a speech in a foreign language to a deaf camel, Moses began listing his accomplishments.

"I believe, Fred, that since my last review, I have taken the core goals identified in our department's mission statement and applied them successfully to my own job-specific deliverables. This has obviously been a challenging year, with redundancies and restructuring and the radical realignment of skill sets. However, I have remained a pivotal player, bringing proactive solutions to the party."

Part of Moses was patting himself on the back as he spoke. The rest of him was throwing up. But he had learnt the code. He knew how Fred wanted his words salted.

The creative visualisation was beginning to work. In the back of Moses's mind, a mental image was forming while he talked. He saw a squirrel carrying a bulky sack. The squirrel was standing in front of a giant Oxford teddy bear. The teddy bear looked frightened.

The squirrel emptied the sack, revealing a large pile of coconuts. The teddy bear started to cry. The squirrel was laughing and began pelting the teddy bear with the coconuts.

Moses had to concentrate on the sound of his own voice to make the image disappear.

"Although I would, of course, be interested in learning about areas where my performance could be enhanced, I really do believe, as I say in my review form, that I have achieved an above-par level of quality and productivity in carrying out my duties."

So quit being a prick and show me some action! This wage freeze is beginning to feel like an Ice Age.

Fred nodded his head. He stared at Moses for some moments, twisting his pen in his hands as he formulated his words.

"Interesting speech, Moses." The contempt had crept back into Fred's voice. "You certainly have tried to take on board at least some of the ideas that we discussed this time last year and have made a recognisable effort to implement them. In many regards, your performance has been, as you say, somewhat above par in certain small aspects. You're probably not a candidate for lateral external movement... just yet."

Moses stared at Fred expectantly, trying to work out whether Fred meant that his job was safe.

"You've successfully identified your tangential involvement in some key projects over the last year and you've adapted well to our aggressive strategy of proactive downsizing and resource redistribution," Fred continued. "You have even managed to curb the more extreme manifestations of your tendency towards paralysis by self-analysis. I'd like to take this opportunity to float that on the table. On the other hand –"

"The other hand?" Moses felt his temperature plummet.

"I do still think that there are issues in the area of nondeliverables. I think we need to discuss some of the more intangible aspects of your performance."

The squirrel stopped flinging coconuts at the teddy bear.

Moses suddenly realised that the window in Fred's office was open. Although the sun was shining outside, he felt a chilly draught coming in and creeping up his spine.

"To be honest," said Fred, leaning forward like a cat about to chew a piece of discarded mouse, "I have concerns about your attitude to the job. You say that you have studied, understood and, on a personal level, implemented our mission statement. That's well and good. But, honestly, do you really care your job?"

"Well…" Moses had to clear his throat before continuing. "Er… I'm afraid that I don't quite follow you."

Moses's brain went into overdrive. He frantically tried to guess exactly what Fred was referring to. The only image his brain threw back was of Natalie and Tony, lying on a bed, naked.

"Well, Moses, if you don't internalise the mission statement, it doesn't really matter how many deliverables you achieve. Because there is no bedrock of commitment at the foundation of your performance.

You must internalise in order to externalise."

Tony was lying on top of Natalie, making love to her. In the background, the squirrel and teddy bear watched them, fascinated.

"How do you mean, Fred?"

"I have noticed a certain nonchalance in your attitude to our products." Fred slowly furrowed his brow before continuing. "Now, listen carefully. I don't want any pushback going forward from you on this. We need to leverage our cutting edge by optimising some intangible resources. We are the Marketing division. We have to make people want to, need to, buy our products. We send out the umbrellas or sunglasses, depending on what the economic climate is. Can we do that if we ourselves do not believe in the product?"

"With all due respect, Fred, I think that you are wrong." *And possibly insane.* "I do believe in the product, be it Dom Acc or DataBasics. I believe that they serve their purpose, more or less. They do what they are supposed to do…" Moses hesitated for some seconds. Then he plunged in. "But, at the same time, I believe that we have to keep things in perspective. Domestic Accountant is not going to formulate a roadmap for world peace, is it? These are just small computer programs."

On the bed, Tony and Natalie twisted their bodies. They were lying side by side.

The teddy bear raised its eyebrows.

"Just small computer programs, Moses?" An edge was beginning to scrape in Fred's voice. "With all due respect, do you think that is the sort of thing you should be writing on your marketing literature? With all due respect, is that how you help to deliver shareholder value?"

Moses tried to keep the tremor out of his voice. He could feel the reins of the conversation slipping out of his hands.

"No, not at all. You said yourself that I write good copy. That doesn't necessarily mean that I have to believe all the... um... hyperbole I use to get the customers' attention."

Natalie was kneeling above Tony. Looking down at him. Twitching her body.

The squirrel wiped some sweat from its brow.

"Moses, how on earth can you market what you do not believe in? What sort of messiah would Jesus Christ have been if –"

"Surely you are not comparing us to Jesus Christ!"

"... if He didn't really care about loving thy neighbour. If He thought the whole forgiveness lark was a bit overrated? Do you see what I'm saying?"

"That we should move into the loaves and fish market and manage the expectations of the multitudes?"

Moses regretted it instantly. The image of Tony and Natalie kept distracting him. He tried to banish them from his mind as he waited for Fred's reaction.

On the bed, Tony and Natalie stopped moving and glanced up.

"Now listen here, Moses!" The scrape was deafening now. "I won't take that sort of insolence from anyone. You waltz around the office every day thinking the job is nothing but a bit of a laugh –"

"Well, I don't think that's a fair –"

"– and that we produce programs that are a joke and then you have the bloody nerve to get sarcastic about it. And this is supposed to be your performance review!" Fred paused to catch his breath. His hand clenched his pen, as if trying to strangle it. "Just what the hell is your problem? Do you want an individualised downsizing? Do you want to make a lateral move to the dole queue?"

My God, he's not threatening to fire me, is he? He couldn't be that vindictive!

Moses knew all too well that anything was possible with Fred. Because reckless incompetence was just one of Fred's flaws. He was also capable of holding grudges for years, even if he sometimes forgot the original reason for the grudge. And he was prone to irrational actions in the fury of the moment. He would think nothing of firing Moses on a whim and would then spend the rest of the day creating a policy-compliant case for dismissing Moses.

"You are blowing this out of all proportion," Moses said in an attempt to pluck his career from the fire. He tried to assert some confidence back into his shattered voice. "All I said was that our programs perform a fairly limited... function... in the greater context of... of things."

Tony and Natalie got up off the bed and walked out of the room, holding hands.

The squirrel threw a tiny coconut at the teddy bear. It bounced harmlessly off the teddy bear's hairy chest.

The teddy bear's eyebrows furrowed.

"I think that it would be best if we terminated the meeting at this point, McNamara." Fred carefully returned the pen to its designated position on the desk. "The company has enough issues on its plate without having to deal with your attitude problems. You're lucky that it's just this meeting that I'm terminating!"

The teddy bear glared down at the squirrel. The squirrel was trembling.

The teddy bear opened its mouth.

Tony and Natalie closed the door behind them, laughing.

The teddy bear began to vomit on the squirrel. Streams of warm coffee and spittle and chewed bread poured out of its mouth, drenching the squirrel.

"Er... Okay... I'll see you later... Just give me a call when you think it's a good time to continue our... em... discussion."

"Close the door on your way out!"

The teddy bear started laughing at the soaking squirrel. The squirrel shook himself dry and slouched away, crying.

"I'll see you later then."

Moses stood up and walked out of Fred's office. He closed the door carefully behind him. Without thinking, he wiped his nose, to make sure that it wasn't bleeding.

He wished Natalie would be waiting for him at the cubicle. But he knew there'd be no one waiting except the teddy bear.

The demons were busy with the tricks they taught her,
Working their magic on the fisherman's daughter.
I spoke my mind, I broke my heart,
I watched the whole thing fall apart.
I burned the bridges and poisoned the water,
No shadow could follow the fisherman's daughter.

Blues From A Fisherman's Daughter
Fingers Flaherty

Chapter 2

The Banjo's Got The Blues

I feel like everything I've touched has crumbled in my hands,
Shadows cover the fields where I once stood.
Nothing I believed in has passed the test.
I'd rewrite every damn page if I could.
A hearty meal is a condemned man's last sight.
Nothing for me but the Vacant Blues tonight!

Vacant Blues
Fingers Flaherty

Disjointed conversation rattled the early evening air of Murphy's bar. In a corner, some girls were having a small freewheeling party. At the bar, a group of middle-aged men watched them with interest. From the speakers, Elvis's "Teddy Bear" struggled to be heard.

Murphy's Bar always attracted a mixed crowd. Elderly businessmen mingled easily with college students. Goths shared jokes with HR managers. Builders and hairdressers elbowed each other at the bar. As a result, the manager was never sure how to decorate the place. Some corners were hidden behind rich velvet curtains and ambient lighting. Others were scruffy and indie. The back room could pass itself off as a small conference room. Posters of Bogart, Behan and Beyoncé dotted the walls.

Jesse Conway and Moses shuddered as Elvis's voice ricocheted around the bar. If anything could ruin their enjoyment of their beers, it was the Memphis Flash.

"Nice to see Murphy keeping up with the latest music trends," Jesse grumbled. "He'll probably be playing Brendan Bowyer next!"

Moses laughed. He always enjoyed Jesse's irritability. It helped take his mind off his own niggling annoyances. Even though Moses was forty years younger than Jesse, they had been firm friends for a few years now. They both lived in Ellington Court and had shared many beers together over the years. Although Jesse was spending a lot more time his neighbour Lucy, he still made time to meet Moses every Thursday evening for a few drinks and a rant about the latest irritations.

"Not everyone can have great taste in music, I suppose," Moses conceded.

"Tell me about it! We both remember how horrific your tastes were before I introduced you to the blues."

"Yeah, that was a great favour to do anybody. Add a bit more misery into their life!"

In fact, Moses had learned a lot from Jesse. He'd learned how to keep things in a reasonable perspective. He'd learned to look at the bigger picture, no matter how disheartening the bigger picture was. He'd learned to ignore the thunder on the mountain. And he'd learned that Fingers Flaherty understood him better than anyone else did.

Enjoying the easy silence between him and Jesse, Moses began to relax. He'd recovered somewhat from the trauma of the performance review. He was determined to put it all behind him and enjoy the evening.

Then he noticed Tony Lyons sitting at a far table. He was with a group of accountants from work. The four lads seemed to be, judging by the number of bottles of wine on their table, setting up for a night on the town.

Tony was staring at a young barmaid over in the corner. He said something to the lads and they all exploded laughing.

"Do you know what Fred tried to tell me?" Moses said, as Johnny Ace's "Pledging My Love" began playing. "He tried to compare marketing to Jesus Christ's parables. Jesus Christ was God's marketing agent on earth. That's his way of dealing with our cash-flow crisis. After a one thousand year recession, the messiah will come with his trumpets and stock options."

"There might be something in that." Jesse laughed, dabbing a napkin on his lips. "Aren't the Gospels the greatest ad copy ever written? Raising Lazarus from the dead. That's one way to ensure a loyal market segment. The Sermon on the Mount. What a great way to get the message on to the street!"

The girls in the corner were laughing loudly at a story one of them was telling. One girl was wearing dark blue jeans and a light blue top with an image of the alien from the old *Space Invaders* arcade game on it. Her hands fidgeted with her long blonde hair.

"Well, if Jesus were around now," Moses smiled, glancing over at the party girls, "I don't think he'd rely on our Marketing division to spread his message. He'd still be working as a carpenter in Nazareth if he did."

"Of course he wouldn't! He'd be a syndicated TV evangelist. He'd be trending daily on Twitter. And he'd be curing lepers on YouTube."

Jesse knew all about advertising strategies. He'd spent many lost years writing copy on Madison Avenue. The job had crushed him. Now he found it hard to believe in anything anymore.

"Marketing's all bullshit when you think about it, Moses." Jesse took a quick sip of beer and wallowed in the taste for some seconds. "One day, your product is the hot new thing; next day, it's a bullshit joke. The hypermarket is nothing but a dimestore."

"I know." Moses nodded. "That's what I was trying to tell Fred earlier when I –"

"Once you realise that, everything goes to hell!" Jesse's fingers tightened on his bottle of beer. "You realise that you're nothing but a whore…"

Moses looked around the bar while Jesse drifted off into his memories. Memories of the awful years when he worked for Albert & Stone in New York. Memories of when his life fell apart and he fled to Dublin in order to rebuild himself.

Tony Lyons called the young barmaid over and began flirting with her. She dutifully laughed along with him. The other lads at the table smiled at them. Tony let his right hand slide down her thigh. She stopped laughing and walked away, furious. Tony grinned after her.

"Moses, are you even listening to me?"

"Of course I am, Jesse… What were you saying?"

Over by the bar, one of the middle-aged men, a man with a moustache, was staring at the girls in the corner. The other two men were laughing at him.

Moses was vaguely aware that Jesse was still talking.

The bar manager went over to Tony's table. He asked the lads, firmly, to keep their hands to themselves. The four men protested that they weren't doing any harm, that they were just having a laugh and enjoying their drinks. The manager told them that if they said another word, he'd throw all four of them out and feed them to the greyhounds.

The young barmaid walked past their table and scowled at Tony.

"Do you see that big, long, underfed, lanky, bandy-legged, ugly rake of a thing?" Moses asked Jesse, nodding in Tony's direction

"I knew you weren't listening to me!"

"Do you see him or not?"

"I presume," said Jesse, glancing around, "that you're referring to the tall, young, handsome man in the light grey suit."

"Handsome? He's so ugly, not even the tide would take him out!"

"What about him?"

"That's who Natalie is going out with now. Can you believe that? She left me for that skinny monstrosity!"

"I can't believe you're still harping on about her. She's been gone for weeks now."

"Let's move on to something else then." Moses shrugged. "Tell me, when did you last see a squirrel?"

"What have squirrels got to do with anything?"

"I saw one walking into… I saw one when I was walking into work this morning."

"Really?" Jesse seemed to be utterly lost for words. "Fancy that."

"They're funny little creatures, aren't they?"

"Em… well… yes… I suppose they are… um… when you think about it…"

Tom Jones bellowed "It's Not Unusual" from the speakers.

Moustache was now dancing in front of the girls, while his two friends looked on. The girls were laughing. Space Invader egged him on.

Moses began eating his crisps. In order to distract his mind from Natalie and Tony, he tried to concentrate on the flavour. The salt. The vinegar.

Natalie always preferred cheese and onion.

Over on the dancefloor, Moustache was finishing his dance routine. Space Invader applauded him as he walked away. He turned around and smiled at her, taking a bow. His face was sweating and he looked to be out of breath. He experimented with some jelly jive in time with Tom Jones's roaring.

Space Invader raised her eyebrow and looked away. She got up to go to the bar.

Jesse had slipped off into his own world again. He idly prodded the crumpled crisp packet around the table.

"Listen, Jesse, I'm going to go over to these girls over here for a while. They look like they might be in the mood for… for some fun"

Jesse didn't even seem to notice Moses getting up from the table.

Moses went over to the bar and smiled at Space Invader.

"Hi there. My name's Moses."

"So?"

"Well… um… can I… buy you a drink?"

"No!"

"Okay then." *Jesus, trust me to sail straight to the iceberg.* "So, what are you up to? You going anywhere after here?"

"Home." She nodded to her friends. "I'm fed up of –"

"No, wait!" *Why am I yelping?* "Stay a while. We could have a drink and chat and you never know what might —"

"I'm not sure how to say this." She was nodding her head in time to Tom Jones. "I believe in first impressions. I don't see a spark."

"Listen, I swear I'm absolutely adorable once you get to know me. I can create a spark that would power this poxy city for a fortnight."

"I'm just looking for a little sizzle. Not an atomic surge!"

"Okay, look, it might take time for us to... um... And I'm not unstable. However, I can see your first impressions aren't favourable."

"You're very sharp, Sherlock! I'm glad I'm not polishing you."

"You can polish me any time you want to, honey!" *Oh Christ, did I say that out loud?* "I mean, you —"

"I don't want to dash your hopes," Space Invader replied, leaning towards him, "but there are cabbages growing down in the fields in Wexford that have a better chance than you of scoring with me tonight. So, goodbye!"

She walked back to her friends, shaking her head in disbelief.

Moses ordered a beer and glared at his reflection behind the bar.

I can still turn a chat-up into a fuck-up in nine seconds flat. Oh well, at least the night can't get much worse.

"Hey, bud," a voice suddenly said beside him, "I think I recognise you. But I'm so pissed off my tits I can't place you."

Moses looked round. Tony Lyons's flushed face peered back at him.

From the speakers, Frank Sinatra began belting out "I've Got You Under My Skin".

"I'm sure you've seen me around." *God, he really is a big, long, lanky, bandy-legged, ugly rake of a thing.* "We've probably bumped into each other here or —"

"I've got it!" Tony clutched Moses's wrists. "You used to know Nats, didn't you? You're Elijah. Or is it Jeremiah? One of those bloody superheroes."

"I guess so," Moses mumbled. "You're Geoff from HR where she works, I think."

"I'm Tony." He was smirking now. "God, it's gas bumping into you here. Nats was talking about you just the other night. When we were —"

"Listen, it's absolutely great to see you, but I really —"

"She's a great girl, isn't she? Well, she certainly is now. She's worked out a lot of 'issues' these last few weeks. It's always 'issues' with the chicks, isn't it! We've worked on them together, you could say."

"Super." Moses paid the barman and grabbed his beer. He wished he'd ordered a double whiskey. "I'll see you around some —"

"She seems to know what she wants now. She's certainly eager for it. Anyway, I'd better get going. She'll be waiting for me later. And I don't want to keep her waiting too long, if you know what I mean."

Moses walked back to Jesse's table, wishing that Frank Sinatra's voice would drown out Tony's laughter.

Or that Frank's mafia would come into Murphy's and empty their rifles into Tony's drunken body.

It's enough to make you wonder why you get up in the morning.
It's enough to make you wonder why you came into the bar.
It's enough to make you wonder if you ever really knew her.
It's enough to make you wonder who the hell you really are.

I can't even remember which one of us was right.
Nothing for me but the Vacant Blues tonight!

Vacant Blues
Fingers Flaherty

Moses looked out the window at the darkening sky. The lights were all coming on across Ellington Court. A gentle evening chill rustled the leaves.

Moses had moved into Ellington House four years ago. It was a large, whitewashed house in Dalesborough, one of Dublin's less demented suburbs. The red paint on the window sills was chipped. The slates on the roof looked grey. Tufts of unshaven moss dotted the walls. Beneath its scruffy exterior, however, beat a welcoming heart for its tenants.

There were four apartments in Ellington House. Moses lived on the upper floor, across the hall from Bill and Tiffany. Jesse Conway lived in the apartment below Moses. The other apartment, below Bill and Tiffany, was occupied by Lucy O'Shea.

Moses's apartment was not luxurious – indeed, it was barely adequate – but it served his modest material needs. And, by giving him the independence he needed to function, it also helped to serve his vast psychological needs. He had been living in Dublin for seven years now. He'd long since escaped his Athlone homestead. Long since escaped his outgrown friends. Long since escaped his father. He had built a new life for himself in Dublin, brick by brick.

He had the heating on in his apartment and the third whiskey and soda was already beginning to warm his blood. On one dilapidated leather armchair, his dilapidated college friend, Banjo Corrigan, was rolling a joint with the precision of an expert.

"Are you sure you don't want to take a few hits from this?" Banjo gasped, holding up the joint. "This is good gear."

"No. I've got poxy work tomorrow." Moses knew that inviting Banjo over on Thursday night was not a good idea. But the encounter with Tony had shaken him and he needed someone to listen to him vent. Banjo was great that way; he could listen to a kettle whistle for hours without interrupting it or passing judgement on it. From any practical point of view, of course, he was about as much use as an ashtray on a motorcycle. "I don't want to be going in with a fuzzy head."

"The whiskey and soda will give you a fuzzy head. A fizzy head, as well."

The clock on the wall said it was 11.30.

Banjo had been in Moses's English class at college. His real name was Henry Corrigan. No one was sure why he was called Banjo. Some said it was because he was constantly strung out. Others attributed it to his love of obscure music.

Moses and Banjo soon became good friends and had shared many pointless adventures together. They had stayed in touch when Moses finally left college. Banjo was still struggling to complete his MA thesis on *Alice in Wonderland*. He had recently decided to change the whole theme of the thesis and examine the book as an exploration of the feminine subconscious. His new title for the thesis was "Alice in Wonderbra".

Banjo looked constantly starved, leading some people to suspect he was dabbling in hard drugs. With his untidy, long black hair and scruffy clothes, he sometimes looked the part. However, his hungry look was usually the result of nothing more sinister than his inability to remember to feed himself.

"So, what's up with you, Moses?" asked Banjo, lighting up the joint. "Have you lost your burning bush again?"

Moses lit a cigarette. He looked admiringly at Banjo's joint; it was rolled almost as tightly as the cigarette. The last time Moses tried to roll a joint, the whole thing collapsed in a ball of flame when he lit it. Instead of getting high, he had ended up with singed lips, thanking God that he didn't have a moustache.

"Where to start?" sighed Moses, blowing a cloud of smoke and sitting down on the other less dilapidated armchair.

"Oh, God! Are we in Edgar Allen Poe drama queen territory? You should remember that any day you can get out of bed is a good day."

"I'm afraid I have higher expectations from life, Banjo."

Fingers Flaherty was singing on the stereo. It was his third album, *Corpus Christopher*, the one he released before giving up and fleeing to America. At the moment, he was complaining that his guardian angel had the blues.

"I had my performance review at work today. That alone was enough to get me lining up the coke." Moses took a mouthful of whiskey and soda, finishing off the glass. "Then, just before that horror was unleashed, I got an e-mail from Natalie. Remember her?"

"The one with the legs?"

"Yes, Banjo, she did possess a pair of functioning legs. They were positioned somewhere between her waist and feet."

"They were a fine set of legs, though," said Banjo, grinning. "What did she have to say for herself? Apart from 'Aren't my legs just fabulous?'"

"Nothing much." Moses angrily stubbed out his cigarette. "Just that it's over between us. Something trivial like that."

"Well, that's not too bad. You knew that already. Just move on to someone else."

"They're not exactly forming a disorderly queue outside my door, are they? I can't help it if I'm always looking for the Promised Land. I mean, there has to be somewhere better than *this*."

"Oh, cheer up, for Christ's sake!" Banjo laughed. "I've had to deal with far worse shit when I've broken up with my girlfriends. I always get the bunny boilers. And the bunny grillers. Bunny blenders. Bunny shredders. Every bunny in the country shits itself when I start going out with someone."

"Anyway, Natalie has decided to go out with Tony Lyons. He's this big, long, underfed, lanky, bandy-legged, ugly rake of a thing who works with her."

"And you're Henry Cavill?"

"That's very helpful, Banjo."

"I'm just being devil's advocate."

"You're just being a prick!"

They fell silent for a while. Banjo finished off his joint and lay back, eyes closed. Moses sipped his drink, wondering what Tony Lyons was doing now.

He could see Tony in some dark kinky nightclub.

Tony is drunk, his eyeballs popping out of their sockets as he scans the room. He sees a girl with her back to him. She's wearing tight white jeans and a loose purple sweater. She has black curly hair. She has a great body, her clothes stretching across her full figure.

Tony stumbles towards her and taps her on the shoulder.

"Hello, babe!" He leers. "You feeling lucky?"

The girl turns round to face Tony.

Tony's face blanches as he yelps.

She's actually a rabid teddy bear.

"Oh, I'm... sorry," stammers Tony, "I... thought... you were someone else."

"Hello, big boy!" The teddy bear smiles. "It's your lucky night."

Before Tony knows what is happening, the teddy bear is kissing him.

"Come with me, Mr Accountant," the teddy bear whispers, "and I'll really balance your books for you."

Tony and the teddy bear walk out of the nightclub, arm in arm.

"Of course," said Moses, blinking his eyes back to reality, "the e-mail was just the first level of hell. The performance review brought it to the next level entirely."

Flaherty's "Bunion Blisterin' Blues" started playing.

Banjo had obviously drifted off to some stoned alternative universe.

"Banjo!"

"What?" Banjo's eyes had the stare of a fish on a slab. "What? What? What?"

"Coconut Fred bawled me out of it. You're lucky you don't have performance reviews in that corner shop where you pretend to work."

"Yeah. We don't have meetings. We have power huddles. I remember one day the boss really read me the riot act during our huddle. It was all meant to be part of my skills development. All I developed was a constant migraine. Anyway, I don't work there anymore. I was downsized with extreme prejudice yesterday."

"What's happened now?"

"I was working the morning shift for a change. This ancient cobweb-infested priest came in and asked for a packet of 'the usual'. I mean, what was I to think? I automatically assumed, like any sensible person with a few scraps of brain to call on, that he was talking about rubbers. A priest can't ask for a pack of balloons, so obviously he'd say 'a pack of the usual', just in case any of his parishioners were in the shop at the time. It made perfect sense to me. So I handed him the packet of condoms."

"And it didn't occur to you that he might be asking for a packet of cigarettes."

"Well, as it turned out, yes, he was actually asking for a pack of twenty Major. But the need to be psychic wasn't listed on my job description."

"Is that why the boss sacked you?"

"No. He just ate me raw over that. He fired me later after I fell asleep over the ham slicer while one of the old bats was rabbiting on about the evils of the youth of today."

"Jesus, Banjo, you've been fired more often than a pistol down in old El Paso."

Moses filled another glass of whiskey and soda. His blood felt warm and relaxed now. He could feel the tension of the day melting inside him.

Banjo was now busy rolling up another joint. Flaherty was telling the story of "Red Wine And Sour Grapes".

Moses's phone started ringing. He reluctantly picked it up.

"Hello?"

"Moses, it's Dad. How are things?"

"I'm fine," Moses lied. "How are things with you?"

"Good. Yes, things are going fine."

"That's great." Moses was still sober enough to sense that his father seemed to be relaxed, but he knew that a few wrong words would set his father off on a biblical rant. "Super. Smashing."

"I was talking to Stephen earlier. He was asking about you."

"Really?" Moses found it difficult to talk about his brother without wanting to strangle some rabbits. "How… is he?"

"He's doing really great, son. He got a nice pay bonus at work last week. His company seems to have survived the credit crunch carnage. He and Krystal are buying a house. He has managed to keep his nest egg safe over the last few years. Unlike most people. Unlike certain people I could –"

"Wonderful!"

"So tell me," Mr Doyle said hesitantly, "how did your performance review go?"

"Yeah, cool." *Good job he can't see how red my face has got.* "The review went… really well."

"You said before that your boss doesn't like you. Are you giving him any reason not to like you?"

"No. None at all."

"I hope not. You have a careless mouth at times, Moses. Is it just a personality clash?"

"I guess so." *Teddy bears and squirrels don't really get along.* "He's under a lot of pressure these days because the sales guys are having trouble selling our shit and they're blaming the marketing people. Any of us could be fired at any minute... But at least the review went... okay... I suppose."

"Just *okay?*" A suspicious edge entered Mr Doyle's voice. "You said a minute ago that it went really well."

"Well... yeah... I mean... it went... fine."

"For God's sake, don't you even remember how it went?"

"It went well!" Moses thought he could feel his brain begin to split open. "I think. I'm not sure yet. It's... not over yet. We have to have a follow-up meeting."

"A follow-up meeting?"

"Oh... er... we didn't... um... finish up all our... stuff."

"Why the hell not?" The biblical rant was tuning up. "You didn't storm out of the meeting, did you? That's you all over. Things don't work out your way so you storm out. Just like a child throwing a tantrum. All the toys come flying out of the pram. You're just going to have to realise that the world doesn't revolve around you, Moses. That's why Natalie left you, of course. You were so self-absorbed that you –"

"I didn't storm out." *Natalie! Natalie! It always comes back to Natalie!*

"We just –"

"If you're not careful, you're going to lose that job. You'll be back at square one again, wasting every day and farting your life away. You don't want to end up like that hopeless Banjo you were with at college, do you?"

"No." Moses wished he was Banjo right now, stoned far away from hectoring fathers and reality in general. "What you don't seem to get is that I'm –"

"If you lose that job, you'll just have to come back home and start working for me. That's the only way I can be sure that you're keeping on top of things."

"I'm not going to lose my job!" The thought of working for his father filled Moses with terror. "Why do you think I'm –?"

"Stephen manages to get through work without throwing knicker fits. Why can't you?"

"He gets lucky. I get shat on." Moses knew he should hang up, but he almost relished entering into battle. "He was obviously born under some lucky star when the church bells were chiming. I was born under a leak."

"Look, it's very simple. Stephen works hard and gets what he deserves. You arse about like a crippled jellyfish and get exactly what you deserve. You're too old for these adolescent dramatics!"

"No matter what I do, you always tell me that Stephen could have done it better." Moses was surprised to find that he was shouting. The whiskey sizzled in his stomach. "I could start raising the dead and you'd phone Lazarus to tell him that Stephen knows how to do it better. All my life, I've tried to please people, but it's just never enough. I'm sick of it. I'm fucking sick of everything!"

Moses switched off his phone.

Banjo was finishing rolling his joint.

"That was Dad," Moses explained, unnecessarily. "We… em… had a bit of a row. About work… And Natalie, I suppose"

Moses sat down in the armchair and drained his glass. He looked at the joint Banjo was working on.

"Give me a few hits off that when you're ready, Banjo. I need something to calm me down."

Moses desperately wanted to get stoned and forget about everything. The whiskey had softened the edges, but it wasn't enough. The edges had to be obliterated. Complete evaporation.

After some minutes, Banjo lit up the joint and passed it over. Moses inhaled deeply and nearly choked when the sharp smoke engulfed his mouth. He'd forgotten how strong rollies could be. He took three gentler hits and passed the joint back to Banjo.

He poured another glass of whiskey and soda as he waited for the smoke to settle in his brain. His vision was already beginning to blur from the whiskey.

They passed the joint back and forth in silence. Moses knew he was inhaling the hash too greedily. He hadn't forgotten that he had work the next morning. He just didn't care anymore.

The two clocks on the wall said it was already 12.00.

Moses stretched out and lay back in the armchair. When he closed his eyes, his eyelids felt as heavy as wet velvet curtains. The hash started fluttering inside him. His mouth felt desert dry, but it was too much effort to reach over for the whiskey bottle.

Flaherty was singing "Dancin' At The Crossroads", one of his more up-tempo numbers. He sounded like he was enjoying singing it.

Moses listened to the song and felt himself very slowly slip away. He wondered what his brain was going to vomit up.

"You can't change the inevitable, Banjo." Moses took another sip of whiskey. His mouth felt cracked and dusty. His hand was beginning to tremble slightly. "When they've built that cross for you, you might as well just climb up on it and get it over with. Come on up and see the view."

"Exactly," said Banjo, after a very long pause. "That's it... exactly... yeah."

As he listened to the song, Moses could clearly see Flaherty in his battered grey suit and straw hat, standing at a deserted crossroads in the middle of some atomic wasteland. Flaherty's voice sounded crisp and distinct; Moses could hear every breath between the words.

Soon the dancers came to the crossroads.

Next came Elvis, dressed all in leather, an advert for his 1968 TV special sewn on his elbows. He was munching a huge hamburger.

There was a huge hollow tree beside the crossroads.

"You know who the greatest entertainers in the world were, Banjo? Jesus, Hitler and Elvis."

"It's a pity only one of them was crucified."

After a minute, everyone climbed into the hollow tree. Moses's eyeballs rolled in after them. The interior of the tree was huge, with rich yellow velvet walls and a black marble floor with gold stripes. A mirrorball hung suspended in the air and spotlights lit up the interior. A huge neon sign proclaimed: "The Hollow Tree Hotel, Las Vegas, presents Fingers Flaherty!"

Tony Lyons and the teddy bear came in next. Tony's clothes were torn and he looked exhausted. The teddy bear was still wearing white jeans and a purple sweater. A cigarette smouldered in the teddy bear's red-lipsticked mouth. It had its arm around Tony, rubbing his shoulder.

Next to come in was a squirrel, wearing black jeans and a red bomber jacket. It had a white balaclava on its head. In its right hand, it held a small baseball bat. "Squirrel Defence League" was stitched on the back of its jacket.

"I'm sick of everything!" The squirrel jumped into the crowd and began indiscriminately swinging its baseball bat. First to go down was Elvis. The teddy bear jumped on the squirrel to protect Tony.

Although no one was listening, Flaherty continued to play his guitar, wildly. When he hit the last chord, an army of space invaders stormed the dance floor, guns blazing.

The tree exploded in a hail of laser blasts as Moses drifted away.

Some time later, he opened his eyes. The light in the sitting room was blinding. The CD clicked off after the last chord faded away.

On the other chair, Banjo was lost to the world. The three spinning clocks on the wall said it was 1.00.

I follow her from darkness into darkness night after night
That woman lit up my life and then she blew my candle out.
She wrote my life story and then I lost the plot.
She changed my mind and then rearranged every tooth in my mouth.
This low-down dirty dog is as high as a kite.
Nothing for me but the Vacant Blues tonight!

Vacant Blues
Fingers Flaherty

Chapter 3

This Squirrel Walks Into A Bar

Woke up this mornin', my woman bit me with her teeth,
Oh Lord, you know I woke up this mornin' and my woman bit me gum-deep with her teeth,
And then she walked all over me with her new boyfriend's feet.
I've got the paranormal paranoia blues.

Paranormal Paranoia Blues
Fingers Flaherty

Moses groaned as a door slammed in the apartment next door. Bill and Tiffany were unfurling their claws, getting ready to start their day and tear each other to shreds.

"Where the hell is my sodding briefcase, Tiffany?" Bill roared. "It's gone missing."

"You should have taken more care of it then!"

Moses lay in his bed, staring at the ceiling, wondering if his headache would be downsized before he got up for work. Assuming he could get up for work. When he'd tried to move his head a few minutes earlier, the room seemed to have tilted violently. It seemed like only fives minutes ago that it was soon after midnight.

"For Christ's sake, Tiffany, I have to find it."

"Oh, shut up, you whinging prick! I've got a blistering hangover."

"Serves you right! I didn't make you drink all that vodka last night, did I?"

"Screw you!"

"Screw yourself, bitch! Where in the name of sweet swinging Jesus did that briefcase go?"

Moses yawned loudly, trying to block out his neighbours' row. He closed his eyes, begging some alien intelligence to transport him to another planet.

"I've found the briefcase, Tiffany! Do you want to know where it was?"

"Who gives a flying fiddler's?"

"I'm going to grab some breakfast then, you sour bitch!"

"Where are the bastard headache tablets?"

"Same place as the briefcase was."

Moses reluctantly decided it was time to try and get up from the bed.

I wanna be your candy man, baby, throw this salty dog a bone.
Baby, let me be your candy man, this salty dog wants a bone.
I can hear you through the wall, honey, you don't need a telephone.
I've got the paranormal paranoia blues.

Paranormal Paranoia Blues
Fingers Flaherty

Half an hour later, Moses staggered down the stairs. Bill was coming down after him, the famous briefcase swinging by his side.

"How are you, Bill?" Moses croaked.

"Absolutely shite!"

Bill was nearly thirty years old and, this morning, every one of those years seemed to have left a fingerprint on his pale, unshaven face. His perpetually uncombed blond curly hair was receding and his short frame was developing middle-age flabbiness. The dark-brown suit looked like it had been dropped on him.

"Wretched head's lifting off me!" Bill's voice sounded like sandpaper. "We went to The Boiled Pig in the city centre last night. Tiffany's crowd had some work party on, celebrating the latest round of redundancies or something ridiculous like that. We didn't leave the pub until 2.00. I'm suffering for it this morning!"

Moses knew all about suffering this morning. They reached the front door of Ellington House. The sun hit Moses like a wet towel in the face when he opened the door.

Bill seemed reluctant to walk out, gazing outside with a condemned man's enthusiasm for the gallows.

"Cheer up, Bill!" Moses tried to gather the strength for the walk to work. "The day can only get better."

"Please, God, let my car be broken down this morning. I'll see you later, Moses."

Moses couldn't help smiling when he heard the Cortina's engine kick into life, all eager to bring Bill to work.

"You treacherous backstabbing bastard!" Bill thumped the steering wheel. "The one bloody morning I didn't want you to start."

Moses glanced at his watch and started walking to work. He wasn't too late yet.

I can hear your yapping, man, it sounds like a new language to me,
Shut up your bloody yapping, man, it sounds like a new language to me.

You'll never talk sense, man, until you're hanging from a gallows tree.
I've got the paranormal paranoia blues.

Paranormal Paranoia Blues
Fingers Flaherty

In spite of a slight nip in the air, it was another bright summer day. Moses tried to imagine all the sun's vitamins rejuvenating his tired bloodstream. By the time he got to the end of Shaw Road, he could feel a thin layer of moisture between his flesh and his clothes.

I wonder how much Bill is suffering.

Moses liked Bill, in a fair-weather sort of way. Bill could be fun sometimes. He had worked for Cumberland Office Supplies for about ten years, starting below the bottom and very slowly working his way a tiny bit up. He had been a travelling sales rep for two years now.

He had told Moses that he had been seduced by every female office receptionist in Dublin. Even some male ones had tried their luck with him, apparently.

One night, Bill had got drunk in Murphy's bar and told Moses about the day he had sex with a receptionist in the toilets of the Keaton Hotel. He went into surreal pornographic detail, which Moses had found disgusting, embarrassing and admittedly intriguing. Bill said that the receptionist was twenty-one years old and very athletic. She looked like a young Julia Roberts with a hint of Grace Jones.

Moses didn't believe a word of it.

Bill and Tiffany had a violent, high-volume relationship. They both seemed to be thrashing against the solidifying of their relationship. But somewhere deep inside them, their hearts were inseparably tangled together.

Ten minutes later, Moses turned the corner into Cartright Road. The security cameras glowered at him. The air was as silent as death.

The heat now felt suffocating. Moses's underclothes were stuck to his skin.

Jesus, all I want to do is lie down on the pavement and go to sleep. Make a lateral move into a parallel universe.

That was when he heard the rustling in the bush.

Moses stopped walking. He remembered the squirrel he'd seen yesterday. The one he wanted to call Ernie. The friendly little squirrel who had smiled sympathetically at him.

The only sound on Cartright Road was the rustling in the bush.

And Moses's nervous, excited breathing.

The squirrel bounded out and landed on the pavement.

Moses's heart leapt with joy, for about a second.

The squirrel stood still, surveying the scene.

Moses stared at the squirrel, open-mouthed, and became convinced that, somewhere in the course of his walk, he had gone completely insane.

The squirrel looked different this morning.

I saw a squirrel walking into work today.

The squirrel was wearing a little navy-blue three-piece suit and a bright red shirt, with a pink-and-black tie. It had shiny black leather shoes with grey laces on its feet. Perched rakishly on its head sat a yellow Elvis Lives baseball cap. The squirrel was carrying an impressive little crocodile-skin briefcase.

Sweat rolled freely down Moses's face now.

The squirrel obviously sensed Moses's stare. It gave a puzzled grunt and looked around. When it saw Moses, its face broke into an eager smile.

"Hiya, Moses! What's the story?"

Jesus Christ, that hash must have been laced with acid last night!

"It's good to see you, bud," the squirrel continued enthusiastically. "I've been waiting for an opportunity to introduce myself."

Moses nervously looked up and down the road, hoping to see a film crew. Cartright Road was as empty and sullen as ever.

"You know," the squirrel said, frowning with sudden concern, "you don't look the Mae West. In fact, if I may say so, I've got decomposed relatives who look better than you do."

"Actually," Moses said, scarcely believing the sound of his own voice, "I feel absolutely terrible. I had too much whiskey last night and I think it has corroded right through my system. I've got an absolute hairless donkey of a hangover."

"Really?" The squirrel raised its little eyebrows. "The old spirits can knock you right off the tracks. The last time I downed a bottle of tequila, I was locked out of my tree for two days."

The squirrel laughed heartily, but Moses didn't see the joke.

"I hate to be rude," Moses said, kissing goodbye to his sanity, "but I'm afraid I don't recognise you. If you don't mind my asking, who are you?"

And where the fuck am I?

"Floyd! The name's Floyd."

The squirrel extended its paw. Groaning inwardly, Moses gingerly stooped down and shook the squirrel's hand.

"Hello, Floyd." The squirrel's paw felt real enough. And the paw shake was firm and enthusiastic. Moses wasn't sure that that was an entirely good sign. "Nice to meet you."

"You know, Moses," the squirrel said with a grimace, flicking its paw in the air, "you're sweating quite heavily. Your hand is absolutely soaking."

"Oh… sorry…"

"Don't worry about it." The squirrel wiped its paw against its thigh. "It's not the end of the world."

It sure as hell feels like it at this minute.

"Well…" started Moses, not certain how he was going to finish the sentence, "it's… um… er… good to see that it's another nice, sunny day. It… ah… well… sort of… like… gives you the heart to go on… If you know what I mean…"

"You look like death thawing out," the squirrel said, taking off its baseball hat and scratching its head. "You haven't even shaved this morning."

You're one to talk, you hairy little fucker!

"Oh, I'll be fine. I'm kind of on friendly terms with my hangover by now."

"That's as may be." Its head obviously scratched to its satisfaction, the squirrel put back on its baseball cap. "But your eyes look like they're about to roll back right down your throat."

In the background, Cartright Road was a silent as a patient gallows.

"I've got a joke for you, Moses. This squirrel walks into a bar, holding his crotch in agony. The barman says, 'Percy, what happened to you?' 'I was on my way home from collecting some food and I was mugged by a badger,' Percy groans. 'Oh really? And did the badger take anything?' 'No,' says Percy, delicately rubbing his crotch, 'it just tried to grab my nuts!' Ha ha ha ha."

Moses gazed blankly at the laughing squirrel. He could not muster up the energy to laugh along, even though he thought the joke had a certain whimsical charm.

"You really need to sleep off whatever's wrong with you," said the squirrel, when it had recovered its composure. "Sweat it out, bud. Assuming you've got any sweat left in you."

Moses felt very light-headed. His heart started thrashing violently inside him.

"Sleep and relax, Moses. You need to lighten up, throw away some of the old baggage. Nobody likes a martyr. That's why all martyrs end up getting killed."

The squirrel's voice sounded like it was coming from outer space. He faded in and out of focus, turning into a red and blue blur.

The world spun violently.

Moses was suddenly looking up into the clear, blue sky. There was only one lonely cloud up there and it retreated from him as he collapsed backwards on to the pavement.

Closing his eyes, Moses let the sun sizzle into him. He desperately wanted to go to sleep.

"Moses! Moses!"

Moses reluctantly opened his eyes. Much to his chagrin, the squirrel was still there, in its navy and red glory.

Okay, this isn't a dream, after all. I'm stuck with it!

Moses slowly raised his head. He eventually pulled himself up into a kneeling position. That seemed far enough for now. His knees felt warm on the pavement.

Jesus, I feel as sick as a small hospital.

"That was some fall you took there, bud. You collapsed quicker than a social media start-up."

"Yeah." Moses stared at the pavement, watching beads of his sweat splash to the ground. "I felt dizzy and the next thing I knew –"

Moses's stomach chose that instant to eject whatever was swilling inside it. A hot, bitter, stinging stream of vomit shot up through Moses's throat and gushed out of his mouth, splashing noisily on to the pavement.

The squirrel managed to leap out of the way just in time.

"Jesus Christ!" Moses moaned, as his bones rattled inside him with every breath. "What the hell is wrong with me?"

"God almighty, Moses!" For the first time, the squirrel sounded irate. "Did you want to drench me in your puke?"

"I'm sorry, Floyd."

The squirrel looked at its watch – a gold watch, no less – and let out a little yelp.

"Oh shit! I didn't realise it was so late. Listen, Moses, I'm going to have to shoot. I'm supposed to be at a time management meeting that started five minutes ago. They'll crucify me for being late… But I really don't like leaving you in this state, bud. You're kneeling in a pool of your own vomit."

"Floyd, thanks a lot for staying with me. I'm going to be fine. Thanks again."

"Well, if you're sure… You take care of yourself." The squirrel picked up its briefcase. "I'll see you soon, Moses."

And with that, the squirrel headed down the road. It scurried into one of the bushes, its tail swishing in the sun.

Moses carefully stood up and shook the vomit off his knees. The sun felt pleasantly warm again. He took his mobile phone out of his pocket and called Fred's number.

Fred's answering machine kicked in after six rings.

"This is Frederick Hearty's phone. I can't take your call right now, but leave a message after the tone and I'll get back to you."

Moses took a deep breath.

"Hello, Fred, it's Moses… I won't… er… be able to make it in today… I'm not feeling well." The image of the squirrel in all its regalia flashed before Moses. "Not well at all."

Moses put the phone back in his pocket.

Cartright Road continued to sternly gaze at him in silence.

Moses started to stumble home.

You know, I been there, done that, taken the medicine,
You know, I been there and I done that and I even taken the medicine,
It's time to dim the lights and praise Thomas Edison.
I've got the paranormal paranoia blues.

Paranormal Paranoia Blues
Fingers Flaherty

It was 7.00 in the evening when Moses finally awoke from his dead sleep. The digits on the electric clock glowed eerily.

Moses gingerly slipped himself into consciousness. The sleep seemed to have done the trick. He almost convinced himself that he felt great. However, in the back of his mind stirred the tiniest doubt about his condition.

He switched on his CD player. The raw opening chords of "Paranormal Paranoia Blues" introduced Flaherty's rant about life's mistreatment of him.

Moses decided it was time to get up. He threw on his dressing gown and sat on the bed for a few seconds, trying to work out his next move.

Peace. Perfect peace. That's about all I'm fit for now.

"I'm home, Tiffany!" Bill bellowed across the hall.

Moses groaned, knowing that the fragile calm that had enveloped him was about to be shattered.

"I'm home, I said. Are you deaf or something? I've had a really shit day. Where the hell are you, Tiffany?"

"I'm in the bath."

"What are you doing in the bath?"

"What in the name of Christ do you think I'm doing in the bath?"

"It's a strange time of the day to be taking a bath. Anyway, I've had a shit day. I was stuck in traffic for two hours."

"Is that all?"

"Jesus Christ, what more do you want? Do you want me to say that I also got molested by a gamey giraffe?"

"At least it might have shut you up!"

"Fine! Well, I'll ring the giraffe embassy first thing in the morning and book an appointment."

"I'm sure you and the long-necked bastard will be very happy together! I might be able to have my bath in peace then."

Moses's phone started ringing.

"Yes?"

"Hiya, Moses," a familiar voice chirped. "It's Floyd."

Moses's sanity made one last desperate attempt to deny what was happening.

"Sorry? Who's this? I think you may have the wrong number."

"It's Floyd, bud. Remember? From this morning?"

"This isn't happening." Moses's sanity fled in retreat. "This is just a dream."

"If it's a dream, I must be having the same one." The squirrel laughed. "Or we're both dreaming someone else's dream. Maybe Elvis is dreaming about us in Las Vegas. Stranger things have happened. Anyhoo, how are you now, Moses?"

"Yes, I'm fine." Moses yawned. "I'm just up out of bed."

"Oh, so you didn't go into work?" Floyd sounded relieved. "That's good. You were fit for nothing but the hay when I saw you this morning."

"I took your advice and went straight home."

What the hell am I doing? Hang up! Slam down the receiver and run back to bed and forget this is happening. You'll wake up in the morning and the world will be tickety-boo again. Or at least as tickety-boo as my world ever gets.

But Moses's hand refused to move. Although his brain was going through a riot, his body felt calm. The squirrel's voice was relaxing, a warm herbal bath pouring out of the receiver.

"When I got back, I just hopped into bed and knocked out all the lights."

"I just wanted to check in with you. I was kind of worried about you all day."

"Thanks!"

"That's what friends are for, bud. Listen, I've got another joke for you. This squirrel walks into a bar and… Shit, that's the one I told you earlier! This squirrel walks into town, his arm in a sling. It's twilight. Only a few people are out walking. A lonesome wind whistles down the street. A tumbleweed rolls into the saloon. A church bell tolls ominously in the distance. The squirrel stands there, his arm in the sling, a mean look in his eyes. Eventually, the sheriff approaches the squirrel. 'What you doing here, pardner?' the sheriff asks. The squirrel points to his sling and says: 'I'm looking for the low-down dirty rat who shot my paw!' Ha ha ha."

"Very cute, Floyd."

"Now, Moses," said the squirrel, "can I ask you a question?"

"Yeah, sure." Moses could feel his headache coming around the circuit again, picking up speed. "Go ahead."

"How are things with you? I mean, beyond the self-inflicted martyr complex, how are you?"

"Er… I'm okayish, I suppose. You saw what I was like this morning."

"What do you know about Elvis, Moses?"

"Enough to know I don't want to know more. What the hell has he got to do with anything?"

"Everything I've learnt in life I've learnt from Elvis. Some people listen to him and hear nothing but white trash hillbilly music –"

"Exactly," Moses agreed.

"But when I listen to him, I hear the rhythm of the jungles. His music reminds me that, for all our civilised ways, we're just wild animals at heart. That's why people were afraid of him, you see. He reminded them of how wild they really were."

"Is there a point to this, Floyd? My brain is too corroded to try and make sense of what –"

"You went a bit wild yourself last night, didn't you?" The squirrel's tone was more concerned than hectoring. "Became a right little hound dog. The ready teddy wanted to rip it up! You got drunk and now you've got a hangover. But that's all only a symptom."

"That's very insightful!" Moses gently eased himself off the bed and down on the bedroom floor. "I never would have worked that out on my own."

"What I mean is that you're not facing up to why you got so drunk. We need to analyse the situation, bud."

"Should I lie down on the couch and start talking about my mother, Dr Freud? Dr Floyd Freud?"

"Moses, you have to face facts here, and I'm trying to help you. But there's only so far I can go. I can't crawl into your head, can I?"

"You're making a damn good attempt at it!"

"Moses, what's really bugging you?"

The bedroom spun gently around Moses. He was suddenly afraid he was going to start crying.

"Everything," Moses moaned.

"Now, we're getting somewhere," the squirrel said, with relief. "Okay, let's try to narrow it down a bit."

"I think that while I was asleep, I had a nervous breakdown and now I've completely lost the plot."

"And why do you think that?"

"Because I'm on the phone talking to a fucking squirrel!"

The only thing that was stopping Moses from screaming was the calm, rational, soothing voice on the other end of the telephone.

"Now, Moses," that calm voice purred, "you know that's not the problem. What has gone wrong lately?"

"My performance review."

"Why?"

"I had an argument with my boss."

"Why?"

"Because he's a vindictive prick!"

"That's not the correct answer, Moses. You're still talking about symptoms. Dig deeper. Look into the jungle. So again, why?"

"I wasn't paying attention. I didn't concentrate on what I was saying."

"Why?"

The phone seemed to be slithering in Moses's sweaty hands.

A vague image began to materialise. Moses knew the answer was in that image. He focused his eyes on it. But the more he concentrated, the vaguer it became.

"I don't know, Floyd."

"You were distracted at your performance review because an image refused to leave your head. The image you're trying to see now."

Moses saw clearly the image that had haunted him during the performance review. Tony and Natalie making love, their bodies jerking and sweating with abandon. Two bodies, wild in the moment. The look on Natalie's ecstatic face. A face from which all memory of Moses was erased.

No sooner did the image become distinct and unmistakable than it suddenly disappeared.

"I'm just staring at a blank wall, Floyd."

"A Zen Buddhist can find enlightenment by staring at a blank wall for hours."

"Well, all I'm seeing is cracks in the plaster."

"Look at the plaster between the cracks. That image is the trigger, Moses. Climb down off your cross and tackle that core problem. Do you remember what you said at your review?"

"No!"

"We have to move into the loaves and fish market. There's a multitude out there, Moses."

With that, Floyd hung up.

"Floyd!"

The phone sat dumbly in Moses's shivering hand. The bedroom felt like a fridge. A cold storage room for frozen loaves and fish.

Moses thought he was made of water. He wanted to lie there forever and slowly seep into the wooden floor.

Maybe he'd wake up reborn tomorrow. He couldn't go on like this. His job was a farce and, even at that, he could barely hold on to it. He was facing the dreadful prospect of having to work for his father in order just to survive.

Worse than all that, Natalie had left him. She was now trying to forget him. And the only way Moses would be able to forget her was if he went back out into the jungle himself. It was time to go hunting.

Actually, given the fragile state of his brain, Moses decided that it was time to go back to bed.

And try not to dream about Natalie.

I can't stop lookin' at my woman, but she plucked out my eyes,
When I was lookin' at my woman, Lord, she turned around and plucked out both my eyes,
Now they're dangling from her earlobes, starin' down at her thighs.
I've got the paranormal paranoia blues.

Paranormal Paranoia Blues
Fingers Flaherty

All Shook Up

Guardian Angel Got The Blues

Bless my soul, what's wrong with me? Am I another lost cause?
What the hell is wrong with me, boss? Am I just a lost cause?
Is Jesus coming across the sand? Is that a banjo in his jaws?
I've just gotta accept there's always something else left to lose.
Tonight, my guardian angel has got the blues.

I said, "Do you mind if I smoke, baby?" She said, "Honey, I don't care
if you burn."
"Do you mind," says I, "if I smoke, honey?" "I don't care, baby," she
says, "if you smoulder up and burn."
My dreams are trying to tell me things I know I can never learn.
Gotta earn your money. Gotta pay your dues.
Tonight, my guardian angel has got the blues.

I'm hangin' around the marketplace, I'm hangin' from the cross.
I was hangin' around the marketplace, now it seems I'm hangin' from
this cross.
Keep rollin' me over, baby, in case I grow some moss.
This train has got no driver, the ships have lost their crews.
Tonight, my guardian angel has got the blues.

Sugar my coffee, baby, won't you butter my bread?
Will you sugar my coffee, do you think you could butter my bread?
She said, "Yes, I will, honey, when I see you dead."

See the flexin' of her muscles as she's tightenin' the screws.

Tonight, my guardian angel has got the blues.

When I took you to a party, you wanted to listen to church bells.

Took you to a rockin' party. All you wanted was the holy church bells.

She showed me a glimpse of heaven, before draggin' us all back down
to hell.

She'd make the Good Samaritan reconsider his views.

Tonight, my guardian angel has got the blues.

Chapter 4

Lazarus On The Pull

Billy's hit the bottle, Bobby's hit the bed,
Baby's gone and hit me until I can't breathe.
Her legs make me go weak at the knees.
I wish to God she was a millipede.
I'd climb out of my grave to be her ghost.
The Loser Blues have always hurt me the most.

Loser Blues
Fingers Flaherty

"Lazarus is dead!"

The congregation of St John's church gazed back at Fr Pepper in silence.

"Gone! Shuffled off his mortal coil. Pushing up the daisies. Trying to get to heaven. He is an ex-Lazarus!"

Fr Pepper paused and took a deep breath.

"This guy," Jesse whispered to Moses, "really needs to get some professional help about his death complex. Talk about wailing of worms and tombstones! He won't be so fond of death when he gets to my age."

"Lazarus is on his deathbed," Fr Pepper continued. "His family are gathered around him. They remember the fine, strong man he once was. The life and soul of every party, tearing into the wine and bursting into song. Dancing naked in the market square at four o'clock in the morning, his underclothes wrapped around his head."

Moses stared at Fr Pepper, wondering where this sermon was going and wondering when it would be over.

"But Lazarus isn't crying, my dear people. In fact, he is quite calm. And why do you think that is?"

Somebody coughed.

A baby gurgled.

"Why? Because he has been through this before. About thirty years ago, Jesus came in and raised him from the dead. Lazarus had felt strange for a few days after that," Fr Pepper continued. "But soon he was out partying again, drinking and singing and frightening the nice women in market square at four o'clock in the morning."

I could do with the Lazarus touch these days. It might bring my sex life back to life, if nothing else. It might help me to… Maybe I shouldn't be thinking about this in church.

Sometimes, sitting in St John's chapel, Moses found himself thinking of when his father and mother used bring Stephen and him to the small parish church back home to listen to old Fr John Murphy furiously preach. Back when he could sit in the same room as Stephen without wanting to commit random murder.

"And so, when the bony hand came knocking to his door, Lazarus believed it was only going to be a temporary inconvenience. But, as he died, he couldn't help wondering why Jesus hadn't turned up yet. His friends politely reminded him that Jesus had been crucified many years ago."

Fr Pepper wiped some Catholic sweat from his brow.

A baby started crying in the back of the church.

"Poor old Lazarus is getting deader by the minute. Picture the scene. Visualise it clearly."

Moses winced, thinking about Natalie's visualisation excesses.

"Focus on the details. The family starts thinking about the funeral arrangements. And, when no one is looking, they stare outside, searching for Jesus. But the sun eventually packs up its tent and the stars start crawling out of their caves. In the market square, lamps are lit. And in the bedroom, Lazarus is as dead as ever."

It's not just my sex life that needs to be resurrected. My career is fairly dead in the water too after that shambles of a performance review. Not too hard to visualise where I'm heading! The dole queue or my father's office. I'm not even sure which one is worse.

Lucy was sitting a few rows in front of Moses. She seemed to be paying close attention to Fr Pepper.

An embarrassed woman carried the crying baby out of the church.

"Lazarus was dead and would stay that way. Just like all the other people Jesus had performed miracles on. The lepers. The blind. The paralysed. Like Lazarus, they all died. Eventually."

Fr Pepper squinted his eyes against the glare of the sun. Although about forty, with greying hair, he had the youthful sense of humour of all New Age enthusiasts. He often started his sermons with a harmless joke. He never condemned anyone from the pulpit. Instead, he focused on the warmer aspects of Christianity. Things such as forgiveness, compassion and love of the outcast. The trendy, politically correct aspects of the dogma, the cynics sniffed.

"Acceptance! That is what I am talking about this morning. We ask

God to give us a break. Instead, we should be asking for the strength to deal with the breaks we've got. The strength to accept what we can't change. Acceptance. Accept the life you're living."

Not everyone liked Fr Pepper, of course. Some of the older people thought him a bit too "modern" or "fluffy", a talk-show priest. They harked back to the dogmatic days of fire and brimstone, when everything was black and white, and Fr Murphy condemned everyone from the pulpit.

Some other people didn't trust Fr Pepper. They thought he was just a little bit too sweet to be wholesome. Inevitably, numerous rumours grew up around him. Fr Pepper took absolutely no notice of any of the rumours. He just carried on with his job, ignoring them all.

Moses admired him for that.

"That was the lesson Lazarus's family had to learn. They had to accept that there wasn't going to be another miracle. We have to accept the present moment and live in it. You see, my dear people, we all carry our little crosses around with us. Today, let us pray to God that He gives us the strength to carry our crosses. Pray that God will give you the strength to endure life's little slings and arrows."

Crosses. Slings. Arrows. Got my fair share of those bastards lately! Natalie. Dad. Fred. Myself. But maybe if I can resurrect my career, I can resurrect everything else as well. Maybe then Natalie will reconsider…

Moses stood up with the rest of the congregation to recite the Apostolic Creed.

I have to accept that I'll be hanging around,
I'd swing from a tree to be where she's at.

It tears my heart apart when her fingers scratch my back,
I wish sometimes, oh Lord, that she was a Cheshire cat.
She spread her love on me like butter on my toast.
The Loser Blues always find somebody to roast.

Loser Blues
Fingers Flaherty

Moses bumped into Lucy at the Ellington House car park that afternoon. She was wearing a sharp dark green business suit and white blouse. Her short black hair gleamed in the sunlight. She smiled when she saw Moses.

I think I can see why Jesse likes you, Lucy!

"Hello, Moses," she said. "I'm glad I bumped into you. I'm thinking of having a small party in my apartment on Friday evening. You're more than welcome to come along."

"A party?" Moses imagined Lucy dancing on a table, bottle of vodka in one hand and a king-sized joint in the other, Bob Marley's "Exodus" blasting on the stereo. "Cool!"

"Though it's probably not the sort of party you're used to."

"Oh!" Moses dissolved the image. "I see. Any reason for the party?"

"I just thought it would be nice if all of us in the house got together for an evening. Feel free to bring along a friend. Your girlfriend or whatever."

"I don't actually have a girlfriend or whatever at the moment. She... I... um... We... eh... broke up a few weeks ago."

"Oh..." Lucy looked mortified. "Sorry, Moses. She was a really nice young woman."

"Yes, she was." *You've no idea.* "She was… something else."

"I used to bump into her in the corner shop. A real polite, but assertive woman."

"Oh yes, very assertive." Moses couldn't help wincing, thinking about the many times that Natalie had asserted her opinion of him. When assertiveness wasn't enough, various cushions and teddy bears were flung into service. He still missed those missiles. "She always knows who's boss."

"Well, I'm sure she'll go far." Lucy smiled wryly.

"I've got over it by now." *Time to change the subject!* "Is Jesse coming to the party?"

"Yes. He said he'd drop by for a while."

"Good. It'll give him a bit of a lift. He seems very lonely lately, for some reason. Maybe he's had a falling out with Fingers Flaherty."

"Oh well, Dublin can be a lonely city sometimes. It's a… Well, if you don't mind, I must be going, Moses."

Lucy checked her bag to make sure she had everything and, apparently reassured, she walked round the back to her car.

She throws a party at the drop of a hat,
But every night, she reminds me how to really laugh.
I smile as I nibble her perfumed neck,
I wish, oh Lord, that she was a giraffe.
There was an exodus of women down to the coast.
The Loser Blues leave you with nothing to boast.

Loser Blues

Moses always needed a few drinks on a Sunday evening to help him forget that he had work the next day. This evening, he thought he wanted a few drinks on his own. Then the solitude in Murphy's bar began to get on his nerves after a while, so he headed out to the car park for a smoke.

Floyd was waiting for him outside. He smiled a squirrelesque smile as Elvis's "Don't Be Cruel" kicked in on the speakers in Murphy's bar.

"I had a dream last night," Floyd said to Moses, lighting up a cigar. "It was enlightening, in a way."

"I'm sure it was." Moses nodded. He had no intention of sharing the details of his own latest dream. It involved Natalie, Fred, squirrels and frozen Arctic wastes. "Don't feel that you have to tell me all about —"

"I was sitting in Madison Square Garden, New York." Floyd made himself comfortable on a bunch of leaves as he wrapped himself in his anecdote and the cigar smoke. "Most of the people were in their early twenties, with long hair and designer goatees. The air was heaving with marijuana smoke."

"I wish I was heaving with marijuana smoke!"

On the speakers, Elvis begged his woman not to be cruel.

"On stage," Floyd continued, "Elvis was wearing this cream suit and black shirt. He looked so old and was sweating like a river. His haircut made his receding grey hairline all the more noticeable. I could see the microphone tremble in his hand."

"Sounds like one hell of a concert." Moses blew smoke into the evening sky. "I'm really glad I —"

"Poor Elvis looked exhausted." Floyd sadly shook his head. "His voice cracked when he tried to sing 'Blue Moon Of Kentucky'. But the band seemed to be playing a different song. Elvis kept losing his place and forgetting the lyrics. He smiled nervously every now and then, but he looked terrified. The audience was laughing. Many were heckling. 'Go back to Graceland, you pathetic old bastard!' The rest walked out, shaking their heads in disgust."

Floyd gazed into the distance, his paws idly drumming the pub wall.

"I don't see any enlightenment," Moses prompted.

"If you understood Elvis, you might understand yourself," Floyd said, sliding out of his reverie. "We all have to sell ourselves to someone day after day. Elvis always understood how hard it can be keep going on. To climb up on that stage night after night. He made it look effortless. But he knew the pain. He knew how cruel life could be."

"Everyone else seems to find life effortless," Moses grumbled.

"It just looks that way." Floyd waved his cigar as he unfurled his sermon. "Just listen to Elvis there now. Can you hear how Scotty Moore's electric guitar and D. J. Fontana's precise, gentle drum beat guide the song carefully to its completion? Every piece of the song works in perfect harmony. Shorty Long's easy piano runs. Bill Black's steady bass. The Jordanaires nudging the song along, massaging it on its way."

A weary sigh was the only reply Moses could muster.

"And in the centre of it all, listen to that fierce, confident, sneering voice! He makes it all sound so easy and so well planned and –"

"That's my point exactly," Moses interrupted. "Everything is so easy for –"

"That day in New York," the squirrel interrupted in turn, "it had taken Elvis and the band twenty-eight takes to get the song right. To make it sound effortless. Why do you expect life to be easy, Moses? Why do you think you can capture everything in the first take?"

"Everyone else seems to have it easy."

"Nothing is as easy as it seems." Floyd looked up at Moses. "Sometimes people just like to give the impression that it's easy. I mean, look at you! You're slouching there trying to look all cool and nonchalant with your open-necked collar and scuffed jeans, but I bet you spent an hour getting yourself ready to come here tonight."

"I didn't spend an hour getting –"

"You just have to get back in the saddle." Floyd tugged at Moses's jeans to make sure he had his attention. "Look at Elvis. He had to build things back up in 1968. The critics said that he had got lost in a sea of weak movies and watery music. He was in danger of becoming a joke. Did he lie down and die?"

"Unfortunately not!"

"Exactly." Floyd did not sound too angry about the insult. "He went into a TV studio in 1968 and rebuilt himself. He was Lazarus walking out of his tomb. He took all the new-found energy he'd got from the birth of his daughter and blew away everything. There is a lesson there for you."

"I'm not going to be buying a jumpsuit anytime soon, Floyd," Moses said with a laugh as he stamped out his cigarette. "Anyway, I'm going to head back in and enjoy one more pint before heading home."

"Try not to get yourself crucified before the night is done," Floyd answered and scurried off into the evening dusk.

Moses walked back in and ordered another bottle of beer at the bar. The skinny, pale young barman looked like he was just a few minutes from fainting.

Many couples seemed to be easily enjoying the last ebbs of the weekend. Some single guys were chancing their luck with any seemingly available young women while the speakers began playing Ray Charles's "I've Got A Woman".

Smug bastard Ray Charles! Seems like everyone's got a woman except me tonight!

"Why the glum face? You appear to be looking for your false teeth at a walrus convention."

Moses turned around to see who was talking to him. His eyebrows shot up when he saw Space Invader standing there. She looked more terrestrial this evening, wearing blue jeans and light green cardigan. Her face, however, looked no more inviting than it had the last time Moses had seen her.

"Oh, hi." *How long will it take me to fuck this up?* "How are you? Can I get you a drink? Would you like –?"

"Listen," she replied, without the faintest hint of a smile, "don't go getting your hopes up. Or anything else up. I just wanted to explain why I was such a… why I was so rude to you the other evening."

"That was no problem," Moses lied. "I've forgotten about it already."

"My head was wrecked that evening. I'd had a shit day at work and then that tosser with the dancing moustache was just the last straw.

The knives were building up and I had to throw them at someone. You just happened to be there, that's all."

"Are you sure I can't get you a drink?" Moses paid the barman for his beer. "Look, I don't even know your name."

"I'm sure you can't buy me a drink." Still no smile. "I'm Rita, by the way. My friends call me Razor… You can call me Rita."

"And you can call me anything you like!" Moses grinned, trying to ignore the look the barman was giving him. "Just don't call me too early in the morning!"

"Listen, sunshine," she replied. "I'll never be talking to you early in the morning. Anyway, I just wanted to let you –"

"There's no need to rush off yet. I don't have the plague. As far as I know. Perhaps we could –"

"Okay, let me be clear. You're simply not my type. I like my men to have a bit more pizzazz. And I've eaten sandwiches that have more pizzazz than you."

"I'm not a sandwich!" Moses saw the barman smirking at him now. "You can think of me as a five-course meal."

As Lou Reed's "Walk On The Wild Side" began playing, Moses knew he should run from the battlefield back home. All the happy couples seemed to be getting happier by the minute. More and more single guys were laughing with the women. Moses didn't want to be the only loser on the field.

"You know, Rita," he said, "you've got a real sharp way with words. You could easily hurt someone with that tongue of yours."

"I don't aim to hurt people." Rita was looking around the bar now, obviously bored with the conversation. "I aim to talk straight to them.

And you can't make an omelette without breaking a few eggs."

"Yeah, but that doesn't mean you have to blow up the hen while you're at it! Not unless you want the feathers, of course. But why you'd want feathers with your omelette is beyond me."

"You know, you really should lay off that beer." Rita turned to go to the door. "It's obviously corroding your brain cells."

"Have you considered the possibility that you're about to walk away from your one chance at true happiness?"

"Have you considered the possibility that you're a retard?" She turned back to look at him. "Just forget about it, sunshine. It isn't going to happen with us. Oh, turn off that drowning puppy look! You can't be that desperate. You'll meet someone."

"I think all the asylums are closed for the evening."

"Actually, I think my flatmate might like you." For the first time, Rita allowed herself a tiny smile. "She's looking for a soul companion of sorts… And her standards aren't too high. She kinda likes charity cases."

As Moses watched Rita walk out the door, he wondered why everyone else in the bar seemed to be having such an enjoyable evening. Why couldn't he accept that he'd never find perfect happiness? But he couldn't accept that his job would never fulfil him. He couldn't accept that he'd never satisfy his father. He couldn't accept that some slings and arrows just can't be avoided.

Natalie never accepted second-best. Why should I have to?

As he glared into his beer bottle, Moses realised that the first thing he'd have to accept was that maybe Natalie wasn't going to come back to him.

Money can't buy me love, but it buys her new shoes.
Sex is costin' me, but she sure ain't no whore.
She licks my teeth, her tongue tickles my throat,
I sometimes wish she was a Labrador.
There's a space invader sitting on my lamppost,
The Loser Blues have given up the ghost.

Loser Blues
Fingers Flaherty

Chapter 5

The Sweet Stench Of Success

Sweatin' for my wicked wife
All night between the sheets.
Sweatin' for her all the next day
As I hop around the streets.
Gotta earn more money, Lord,
Sell myself into disgrace.
Ashes on my tongue, dust on my teeth,
Closin' my eyes, kissin' the coal face.

Coal Face Blues
Fingers Flaherty

"I'm beginning to wonder why the hell I even bother getting up in the morning," grumbled Paul Ryan, buttering his scone. He let out another death-valley sigh. "Nothing but mixed-up confusion. I'd have a more meaningful life if I were lying pickled in a jar."

"You spend your life lying pickled in a bar," Roger replied. "No wonder your career path is a barren roundabout. Take responsibility for your life, for God's sake. Otherwise you'll end up like Moses!"

The Aztech canteen was getting busy this Wednesday morning. Moses sat with Paul and Roger at the table by the window. Rays of sun bounced off Paul's face, spotlighting his stubbled, dark mood. By contrast, Roger Flanaghan looked like he owned the world and was happy with the responsibility.

"You're looking rather sharp today, Roger," Moses said. "Who are you trying to impress with the new tan suit?"

"The white shirt goes well with it, don't you think?" Roger smirked. "Certainly better than bright green with dark blue."

"I'm happy with my green shirt." *I knew this stupid bastard of a shirt was a mistake!* "It's cutting-edge fashion."

"More like frayed-edge fashion! I put a bit of thought into how I dress. My socks complement my suit. Your socks don't even complement each other."

"You know, Roger," Paul replied, "I'm sure my dog vomited up the same shade as your suit last night."

"Speaking of dog's vomit," said Moses, "I wonder what soup they have on for lunch today."

"Whatever they can scrape out of the drains, I suppose." Paul grimaced. "You could dissolve a skeleton in that shite they slopped out to us yesterday."

Paul munched on his toast, tiny squirts of marmalade shooting out the side of his mouth and crash-landing on his chin. Roger examined his reflection in a spoon.

Like Paul, Moses was in the throes of a mushy hangover. After getting scalded again by Rita on Sunday night, he'd vowed to stay away from pubs for at least a month. He'd lasted one day. On Tuesday afternoon, he'd phoned Banjo and tore up the town that night. Now, the morning after gleefully tore him up in return.

He winced as he tried to negotiate a large piece of scone down his throat without ripping his lungs. The chef appeared to have mixed raisins, currants and barbed wire in with the dough.

"I take a lot of pride in how I appear." Roger obviously didn't care if they were listening. "If you look professional on the outside, people will assume that you're professional on the inside. You wouldn't eat an apple if the skin was bruised. You wouldn't –"

"Surely to God," Moses said, frog-marching the piece of scone down the last few centimetres of its journey, "that's a bottle of bullshit. They always say that the clothes don't make the man. Or the moron."

"And you can't make a gold necklace out of a cat's tail," said Paul, with the air of Solomon delivering the wisdom of God. "Well, you could try, but the cat wouldn't be too happy. Unless it was allowed to wear the necklace, I suppose."

"I can see that neither of you is having a lucid morning." Roger glared at them. "The reason why I'm wearing a new suit and shirt today is because I have to give an important presentation to some clients this afternoon. This is the time to impress if you want to avoid the chop next quarter."

"You know your problem, Roger?" Moses swallowed another piece of thoroughly chewed scone. "You've forgotten what you're selling. You're supposed to be selling software. That's all."

"Did you smoke too many funny fags last night? That might explain the green shirt."

"You just don't see it, do you?" Moses smiled, shaking his head. "Explain it to him, Paul."

"Well, I would if I could," Paul said, rubbing the marmalade from his chin, "but I haven't a clue what you're talking about. You kind of lost me after... well, after you started talking."

"It's perfectly simple." Moses adopted his patient pontiff tone.

"What you're actually selling, Roger, is yourself. You're just a corporate whore. You're wearing your fuck-me suit."

"With matching fuck-me shirt," quipped Paul, smiling for the first time in two weeks.

Roger glared at Moses for some seconds, gently tapping his spoon on the table. His cereal dissolved into the milk in his bowl, forgotten.

"I can see you'll go far in this department, Moses," he eventually said, a slight quiver on the edge of his words. "This department is perfectly suited to someone who hasn't a clue about marketing. It's a good job Fred's giving us a presentation on this very subject this afternoon. If I'm a whore, then we're all whores. We're all playing the same game. That's how you become successful. That's how you get promoted. That's how you impress people that matter to you… That's how you impress your girlfriend."

Moses knew that he could never become a corporate whore, because he had seen what that had done to Jesse.

Surely Natalie wouldn't want me to be a whore. What if I sold myself to her? Would she buy me?

Roger stood up and picked up his cereal bowl and glass.

"Anyway," he said, "I've got a busy day ahead of me. You never know when lay-offs might be suddenly announced. So long, fellow whores."

"I suppose I'd better go too," Paul moaned, standing up. "I have to finish that report that was due last Monday. Thankfully, Fred seems to have forgotten about it for now."

For Moses, it was still far too early to even think about venturing back into his cubicle. He sat back and began sipping on his scalding coffee. Fred wanted him to write a report on the latest Domestic Accountant customer survey, but that could wait. Fred was probably engulfed in some new high-level fire and had forgotten all about it by now anyway.

He noticed Sandra talking to Roger at the canteen door. Roger seemed anxious to get back to his work. Sandra seemed anxious to get away from hers.

Realising that Roger wasn't going to participate in her work-avoidance project, Sandra turned her attention to a more willing team mate.

"Up to your eyeballs as usual, Moses," she said, sitting down beside him. "Good job the bottom line isn't relying on you."

"I seem to spend my day on the bottom line of this company," Moses replied. "That's what Roger thinks anyway. The prick!"

"Well, you're not exactly soaring the corporate heights, are you?" Sandra sipped her bottled water. "No, this time, for once, Roger seems to be right. I suppose everyone has to be right one day, eventually. I'm sure your day will come… some time."

"I thought you absolutely despised Roger." Moses felt his unreliable gossip antennae twitching. "You once called him the worst brown-nosing scumbag that ever walked on two legs. Is there a thaw on?"

"As usual, Moses, you're completely wrong." Sandra looked everywhere except at Moses. "Roger is a total knob. Unfortunately, guys who are worth looking at usually are. Anyway, that's not –"

"So you think he's worth looking at?" *God almighty, Roger and Sandra would make some couple. Their children would destroy the nation!* "Maybe you need to get your eyes tested."

"Guys who look any way presentable are usually self-absorbed assholes, inconsiderate dickheads or wilting pansies who run back to their mammies or their boyfriends at the first sign of trouble." Sandra shuddered. "Toxic wankers, the lot of them!"

"Jesus, that's some analysis." Moses couldn't help laughing. "Which category do you put me into?"

"You're no way presentable, so you don't have to worry." Sandra seemed anxious to change the train of the conversation. "In other news, I was talking to your Natalie yesterday evening. Well, she's not your Natalie any more, is she?"

"Here." Moses handed her the salt cellar. He no longer felt like laughing. "I'll find a few more wounds that you can rub this into."

"She was at the yoga class…"

"You go to yoga?!"

"Have you got a problem with that?"

"Well, it's just…" Moses drank his coffee. He tried to choose his words carefully, then gave up. "You're not exactly a great advert for yoga, are you? You're the most stressed-out, brittle person I know. A car bomb has more inner calm than you do!"

"Natalie was looking was really well. Much better than she did when she was with you." Sandra could always find an effective response to any attack. "She certainly has some inner calm. That new boyfriend who picked her up after the class was kind of fit, in a rugged donkey sort of way."

"What? That big, long, underfed, lanky, bandy-legged, ugly rake of a thing?" Moses glared into the empty coffee cup. "I've seen better-looking sweeping brushes!"

"Well, he's certainly swept her off her feet." Sandra stood up. "Let's go, Mr Motivation. We'll need to get a little bit of work done today before Fred unleashes his pep talk on us later. Jesus, when he gets on a roll, all I can think about is stapling his lips together and pushing him into the shredding machine."

"You really should consider getting your money back from that yoga instructor," Moses replied, as he followed her out of the canteen. He was alarmed to discover that they were the last two to leave. "You'll need all your inner calm to get through that meeting. Though you can always just spend your time gazing lovingly at Roger and making –"

Sandra let the canteen door close on Moses's face.

The wife, she wants her fancy clothes,
They cost a bloody arm and a leg.
But I'd sell everything for that woman,
Even if I have to beg.
Gotta get flush to buy it, Lord,
Her champagne bath and silicon lace.
I wish I could spend my whole day doing nothing,
Instead of down here all day, kissin' the coal face.

Coal Face Blues
Fingers Flaherty

Moses was late for the meeting, of course. Ever since the performance review, he never relished setting foot in Fred's office. He slipped into the seat between Paul and Sandra, hoping no one noticed him. Paul certainly didn't. He was scrolling down his phone screen, like a reluctant bulldog typing its last will and testament from its death kennel. His fingers tapped the screen in the dirge rhythm of a funeral march.

Moses felt sorry for Paul, in a superficial way. He remembered what it was like to join Aztech and try to come to terms with its chirpy, evangelical corporate culture. He had spent his first three months in the company praying that his recruitment agency would phone him back and tell him that they'd made a terrible mistake, that he should be working for some cutting-edge games company beside the red-light district in Paris. But the phone call never came. The light stayed red and he'd stayed there ever since. And he eventually did get used to it, in some ways.

Lydia and Roger were sitting on the other side of the table. Only Roger seemed happy to be there.

Fred was intensely tapping some keys on his tablet as the presentation screen on his wall flickered chaotically into life. The title slide appeared. "Trending in the Cloud: Aztech Goes Viral".

"Good afternoon, all," Fred said. "Especially to those of you who've only just now decided to join us! As the company organically develops going forward, I thought it would be a good idea to remind you all of what we do here. We need to align our core values with the shifting contemporary landscape. I suppose the best place to start is by looking at our mission statement. It is 'To convert the intangible quality of our product into a tangible, visible market position in an aggressive, competitive economic environment'. That, in a nutshell, is our goal."

The department's mission statement appeared in flashing black text on a garish purple background. Moses's hangover slithered to new depths.

"You'd think he was delivering the Sermon on the Mount," whispered Sandra. "Blessed are the poor sods who buy our crap for they shall raise our fragile share price."

"Fred does have a Jesus complex," Moses agreed. "He gets quite evangelical about our marketing strategy."

"A Jesus complex?" Sandra raised her eyebrows. "Does that mean we can crucify him? I must check to see if I've got any spare nails back at my desk. Why the hell is he waffling on about all this crap now?"

"He seems to think that our company is entering its next phase."

"The same way the *Titanic* entered its next phase when it hit that iceberg. And all we're doing is washing the deckchairs."

"We don't have any deckchairs to wash," Moses said. "They were downsized in the last round of strategic rationalisation."

Fred was slowly making his way through the slides. The slides were a series of increasingly incomprehensible bulleted lists about social engagement, real-time actualisation, virtual warehouses, viral paradigms and instant manifestation. A chair creaked. Roger noisily scratched his leg. Paul was unsuccessfully stifling a hungover yawn. Lydia sighed loudly as she scrutinised her fingernails.

"To be blunt," Fred said, "we must succeed in this changing environment. We must be holding the oar when the goal posts change. Never mind that life coach nonsense about participation being as important as winning. Humans are biologically attracted to the smell of success. Especially in these challenging economic times. And it is up to us to make the sweet smell of success associated with this company absolutely irresistible. You should be able to smell our viral essence all over the Internet!"

"Our products certainly stink," muttered Moses. "This is like a bad trip. Fred must be coked out of his tiny brain. Or else he's been to another management seminar."

"You might think that all that sounds terribly fascist," Fred declared, warming to his secret theme as he paced back and forth. "Sure, the politically correct professors may frown in their cobwebs and scratch their scruffy beards in disagreement. But this theory of success is the spinal message of every philosophy and religion. When Jesus was baptising people, what was the message? What was His market slogan? Follow me and you will enter the kingdom of heaven. Don't follow me, and you'll end up with all the losers in hell. Buy my religion and you will become a success."

Roger seemed to be enthralled by the presentation. He was gently nodding his head in awestruck agreement, eyes alight with evolving revelation. Sandra threw furtive glances in his direction. In the corner. Paul was visibly losing the will to live.

After a few minutes, Fred was beginning to finish his speech with his usual rhetorical flourish.

"That is how we conquer the cloud and begin trending upwards. We leverage our resources to make the market hunger for what we feed it. And going forward, we hope to be in the front line of delivering our quality product to the market, constantly adapting to the evolving environment, optimising our tangible and intangible resources to utilise synergy, pacing our cutting-edge message to the rhythm of the consumers' needs. I'm sure that's all perfectly clear. Now, does anyone have any questions?"

Moses saw Roger raise his hand.

"That was certainly very interesting and insightful," Roger said. "I can safely say that it has helped me clarify and synergise some of my own goals within your department."

"Thank you for saying that, Roger." Fred smiled. "It's always encouraging to receive positive feedback."

"Jesus Christ," Moses whispered, nudging Sandra, "why don't they just jump into bed together and leverage themselves to their hearts' content? This foreplay is excruciating."

Sandra's eyebrows involuntarily shot up at the mention of Roger's foreplay.

"You say that one of the core goals of this company is to become a manifestation of success," Roger continued. "Obviously, we all want to succeed in avoiding the lay-offs. But I was just wondering how you would define this *success*. In other words, what *exactly* do you mean by success?"

"Thank you, Roger." Fred rubbed his hands together, gearing up for another monologue. "You need to understand that 'success' is indeed a key ingredient of our corporate recipe. Think of it as part of the bricks and mortar that make up the silver cloud."

"You mean an underlying philosophy?" Roger enthused.

"Yes! That's it exactly, Roger. You put it nearly better than I could. It is the philosophy that makes all of us – most of us – in this room committed to doing our absolute best to achieve core deliverables. It is a positive, dedicated attitude to the product. A work ethic that is manifest in the quality of the product."

Moses gazed out the window, reluctant to make eye contact with Fred.

"Thank you very much." Roger nodded. "That's certainly clarified it for me. I think I can... Why are you staring at me, Sandra?"

"No reason." Sandra quickly regained her composure. "Actually, I'm just patiently waiting for you to get to the point of your story."

My God, she almost looks embarrassed. I wonder which category she has moved Roger into now.

"Any other questions?" Fred asked, scanning the room.

Moses sensed an almost palpable threat from his colleagues to lynch anyone who dared ask another question. Paul stared longingly out the window. Lydia was already shuffling her blank papers, getting ready to go. Roger was positively beaming with self-confidence.

"Well, then," Fred said, "if there are no more –"

Moses cleared his throat.

"I have a question." *If I'm a success in the office, then maybe I'll be a success in the nightclubs.* "Er... it's about this whole... um... success thing. I'm still a bit... confused about it."

A groan washed over the room. Sandra furiously kicked Moses on the shin, causing him to wince. Roger turned suspicious eyes on Moses.

"Really?" Fred raised his eyebrows and unleashed his stare of death. "Do you not know what success is, Moses?"

"Well, is this success you talk about... is it... qualitative or quantitative?"

"For fuck's sake," Sandra snarled. "What are you playing at?"

"Aren't you talking about two completely different types of success, Fred? Success in the market is quantitative. And to achieve that kind of success... well, quality doesn't really come into it. Isn't it the case that our success depends not on quality, but on how well we prosti... how well we sell ourselves? It really has nothing to do with this holy spirit that makes our job some sort of vocation for the greater good."

"Moses," Fred sighed, brushing some bemused spider off his suit, "where exactly are you going with this? Or are you lost in your own cloud again?"

"Qualitative success does not guarantee quantitative success. This is not a monastery or a political movement. We are ultimately nothing more than... um... slaves to the market."

Fred stared blankly at Moses. The office was silent. "Thank you for that analysis," Fred said, flatly, closing his folder. "It really has helped to... Thanks again for coming."

The room erupted into a relieved chaos of shuffling chairs and sighs and small talk.

My wife, she turned and left me
While I was twistin' in my sleep.
She said I was always lookin' for something,
The golden calf or the lost sheep.
I'll never be a success, I know,
Until I go back to outer space.
I'm trying to do what must be done,
Clenchin' my fist, kissin' the coal face.

Coal Face Blues
Fingers Flaherty

Moses was determined to make a success of his Domestic Account report. He knew that Fred might harbour a grudge over the incident at the meeting. It was time to get what remained of his career back on track. Raise the dead before they got buried forever. Then he might be able to get his life back on track as well.

Just as he was about to lose himself in the report, Moses felt his phone vibrate.

Checking the screen, he saw that Floyd had sent him a video link.

Oh well, the report can wait for a few more minutes.

Soon Elvis was stalking across the screen of Moses's phone. It was a video from the famous 1968 comeback special, when a leather-clad Elvis reinvented himself in front of hungry television cameras. A recent new father, Elvis looked liked he'd finally found a purpose in life again, after years of starring in increasingly limp movies. Smouldering in his leather suit and snarling the words like a caged animal, he reminded viewers why the Memphis Flash had threatened so many people when he'd first sizzled television screens in the 1950s.

Moses watched the video for fifteen minutes before deciding that he had no idea why Floyd had sent it to him. He was about to put the phone away when it started ringing.

"Yes?"

"Hey, Moses!" Floyd sounded as bubbly as a champagne convention. "Did you watch that video?"

"Sure." Moses glanced around to make sure no one was listening to him. It wouldn't do his career path much good if people realised he was talking to a squirrel during work hours. However, everyone appeared to be busy daydreaming the afternoon away. "What was the point of all that?"

"Isn't he fantastic? He looks like he's about to catch fire any minute as he thrashes the guitar and –"

"You'll be catching fire soon if you don't get to the point." For once, work was the priority for Moses. He was determined to get the report finished today. "Why did you send it to me?"

"Isn't it obvious? If you could follow Fr Pepper's pointless sermon, surely you should be able to understand my lesson."

"It wasn't a pointless sermon." Moses always found it hard to resist the lure of a tangent. "Actually, I thought it made perfect sense. We all waste our lives waiting for a miracle, without realising that the real miracle is that –"

"It was defeatist nonsense," Floyd interrupted. "But his hero ended up defeated on a cross, so there's no surprise he'd develop such a wimpy philosophy. Accept what you have and don't complain. That would hardly inspire anybody!"

"I don't think you quite understand what –"

"Did Elvis accept his career in 1968? Did he accept an endless string of movies that even his fans began to mock? Of course not! He cast off his costume and put on a new one. He dressed himself in leather and reinvented himself before millions of shocked eyes. There's a lesson for you in that, Moses."

"I don't have a leather suit."

"You'd look horrific in leather, Moses. That's not the point. The point is you have to dig yourself out of this self-pitying rut you've crawled into and reinvent yourself. Find the spark that once inspired you to go to the office every morning when –"

"I never felt inspired walking into this office," Moses protested.

"Well, you'd better find some inspiration soon. Otherwise, you'll stumble into work some day and Paul will be your boss."

Moses looked at the slouched form in the cubicle across from him. Three empty bottles of water had apparently failed to dilute the horrors of his hangover. Moses couldn't imagine Paul ever being in charge of anything, let alone a department.

"I think it'll be a drunken day in heaven before that ever happens, Floyd."

However, the squirrel had already hung up.

Floyd was right about one thing. Moses did need some inspiration if he was going to finish this report today. It was time to head to the toilet again. He stood up from his desk.

"If you're going for coffee," Paul said, without looking up, "get me one. This DataBasics shit is doing my head in."

"I'm not going for a coffee, Paul. I'm going to take a slash. Would you like me to take one for you too?"

"God, you're too kind! I'll pass. I wouldn't want to take too much out of you."

Moses walked off to the toilets.

He froze when he saw Fred standing at one of the urinals, getting ready to relieve himself. Fred hadn't seen him, his attention taken up with unzipping his fly.

Moses glanced over at the cubicle doors. Both were closed. He had no choice but to go to the urinal beside Fred.

Surely, he's not going to bawl the head off me in the jacks.

Fred glanced around when Moses walked over to the vacant urinal.

"Hello, Moses," he said, tonelessly. "How are you?"

"I'm fine," Moses lied, unzipping slowly.

The only sound was the splash of Fred's urine.

Of all the fucking places to bump into him!

Moses stared straight into the white-tiled wall, getting ready to relieve himself. His heart trembled uneasily.

Beside him, Fred continued to splash aggressively.

Moses's urinal stayed silent. He felt too awkward, and his body refused to help the situation. Thirty seconds ago, his bladder felt like it was about to burst; now nothing flowed inside him.

This is ridiculous! Come on, get it together! Think about waterfalls. Think about Niagara.

Fred zipped up and walked over to the sink. He turned on the water tap.

Moses stood silent, thinking about floods and rain storms and waterfalls and –

"You know, Moses," Fred said, splashing water on his hands, "I was quite taken aback by your question at the meeting today."

Jesus Christ! He wants to hold a fucking conversation!

"Really?" Moses's voice sounded squeaky. He swallowed, but his mouth was as dry as the rest of him. "Why?"

"To be frank, it didn't make any sense." Fred lovingly examined his reflection in the mirror, drying his hands with a paper towel. "I was trying to teach everyone the meaning of success. Your question just confused everyone, including me. How can you expect to become a success if you don't even know what success is?"

"I understand. Well, sorry about any confusion."

"People remember incidents like that when they're deciding which employees to… Well, we'll just put it behind us for now."

"Okay. We'll wash our hands of it, so to speak. Ha ha ha. If you get my… meaning."

"Indeed," said Fred, dryly, as he opened the door. "By the way, does it always take you so bloody long to relieve yourself? No wonder it takes you forever to finish the simplest project!"

Moses's face exploded in crimson embarrassment. He let out a sigh as the door closed after Fred.

His bladder chose this instant to get over its hesitation.

"Success at last," Moses whispered, smiling to himself as his muscles relaxed. "Quantitative and qualitative."

Moses's smile faded when he looked down.

He was urinating on the floor.

I don't want to be your tenant, woman,
I want to be your resident.
I ain't got it up, woman,
Since Truman was the president.
I'm fed up walkin' round, woman,
Livin' out of a suitcase.
Wish you were swingin' here with me, woman,
Holdin' my hand, kissin' the coal face.

Coal Face Blues
Fingers Flaherty

At 5.00, Moses's phone rang.

"Hello? Moses Conway speaking."

"Moses, it's Bill. Listen, can you talk?"

"Yes, ever since I was a little baby sitting on my daddy's knee, actually."

"Don't be so fucking smart! This is serious. I'm in the middle of something here and you might be able to help me. Are you free to talk?"

Moses glanced around the cubicles. Roger and Sandra were off at a meeting. Lydia was listlessly studying a consumer report and her toenails. Paul was tapping away at his keyboard, lost in his own fraught world, searching for a misnamed folder on the tangled network drives.

"Go ahead, Bill. Amaze me!"

"I've just bumped into a hot little one in this here restaurant. I popped in for a drink and got chatting to her. She's a real gamey bird. Twenty-seven years old, ginger hair, freckles, a tight dress that does her body no end of favours. I could marry her and live on an island with her forever, eating nothing but bananas and raspberries. You know the type. She would make a bishop dance in a –"

"Are you drunk?"

"I've had a few brandies, that's all."

"You sound absolutely pissed."

"Never mind that. Anyway, she's mad for it." Bill was now giggling like a love-struck schoolgirl on ecstasy. "And get this! She's a swinger. You know, wife swapping. Her and her husband, some alcoholic journalist… Anyway, it's a numbers game. It takes four to have a successful swing, Moses. That's what she's after."

"Were you sniffing glue while you were knocking back the

brandies?" Moses's head started to spin gently. "What on earth has this got to do with me?"

"Well, Tiffany would shove me backwards through a meat grinder sooner than get involved in something like this. She has absolutely no spirit of adventure, that woman! So I need to find someone to play the part of my wife." Bill hesitated for a moment. "So... I was wondering... um... you know... if you'd... like, I really trust you, Moses... so would you... eh... be willing... to... em... dress up and... pretend to be... my... ahem... wife?"

"What?" *Christ, I wish I was stoned! Then I'd be able to deal with this.* "Are you fucking serious?"

"The four of us could meet in a restaurant later. You pretend to be my wife. They'll take one look at you and, no offence, won't let you next nor near the orgy. That'll just leave the three of us for the orgy and I'll have fun with this bird and –"

"Bill! Bill! Shut up! The glue has stuck to your brain and you have gone insane."

"I'd only need you to sit in on the meeting for fifteen minutes." Bill had his most enthusiastic salesman's voice on. "I'm sure you've been at worse meetings. All you have to do is slap on some make-up, wear a hat, put on a dress and try to look... feminine. And then disappear."

"How can I be the wife? I've got a five o'clock shadow, for Christ's sake!"

"You can shave, can't you?"

"Well, I suppose I could. It'd need to be a very close, clean-cut shave, though. And people have been telling me that I need to reinvent myself." Moses realised his mind was wandering. "What the hell am I saying? Bill, I'm not getting involved in this."

"Come on, Moses, it'd be a laugh. I'm on the chance of the ride of the century. This could be the greatest success since I bumped into those two Egyptian twins at the sales conference. I certainly made those sphinxes smile. You have to be adventurous, Moses. You're not having much luck doing things your way, so let's try my way for a while now. You need to think outside the box."

"You're so far outside the box, you can't even remember what it looks like!"

"Didn't you and Nat every dress up now and then to liven things up?"

"What's this got to do with Natalie?" *Why does Bill even wonder about things like that? I wonder if Natalie still has that nurse's costume I bought her.* "You've no idea what a normal, stable relationship is, do you?"

"Is that what you'd call your relationship with Nat?" Bill started laughing. "Let's be honest, Moses, there was nothing stable about that."

"Goodbye, Bill!"

Moses put down the receiver. He stared into space, trying to get his head around the conversation. He failed, so he turned his attention back to the computer, trying not to think about dresses, hats, electric suits and close shaves.

At 5.30, the Domestic Accountant report was more or less ready. It wasn't perfect, but it was reasonably imperfect.

Good enough is good enough, as mother used to say. I wish my father was as easy to please!

Moses read through it quickly and, deciding that it was above par, went into Fred's office. He hoped this would end the day on a successful note.

He knocked on Fred's door.

"Come in."

Moses strode in and stood before Fred's desk.

"Here's that marketing review you wanted, Fred." Moses didn't try to hide the smugness from his voice. "I hope it has successfully met its objectives."

"Thank you, Moses," Fred said, quickly flicking through the document. "Yes, on first glance, it looks to be... basically... satisfactory... Oh, by the way, did you finally manage to take that leak?"

"I'm sorry?" Moses noticed that Fred was smirking at him. "How do you mean?"

"It's just that you seemed to be having difficulty getting it together in the toilets this afternoon. Did you finally reach the project deliverable?" The rare sound of Fred's laughter filled the office. "Were you ever able to utilise your resources? Or are there problems in that department? Perhaps a resurrection of morale is in order. I'm sure there are pills available for that."

Moses stared at Fred, utterly lost for words. He wanted to disappear into the carpet.

"Goodbye, Fred," Moses stammered, desperate to leave.

"Goodbye, Moses!"

Moses closed the door behind him and walked back to his computer. He switched the machine off and locked the drawers.

It was time to leave the marketplace.

They say it looks like snow,
They say it looks like rain.
They say it looks like
You've left me once again.
My confidence has left me,
Gone without a trace.
I'm just down here day and night,
Wonderin' why I'm kissin' the coal face.

Coal Face Blues
Fingers Flaherty

Chapter 6

The Cemetery Shuffle

Put on the glad rags, put on the spray,
Put on the swagger, put on the sway,
She's tearing off your clothes, she's tearing out your eyes,
The blind-date bedroom holds another surprise.
Enjoy the silence as you play.
There's gonna be a party in the cemetery tonight.

Party In The Cemetery
Fingers Flaherty

In Lucy's sitting room, the Beatles' "Day Tripper" was playing softly, creating a gentle Friday evening ambiance. Lucy, in a dark blue suit and a white blouse, looked slim and lively this evening. She seemed to be engaged in a slightly flirtatious conversation with Jesse. Tiffany was in the kitchen talking to Lucy's niece, Bubbles.

Unlike Moses's apartment, Lucy's was tastefully decorated with subtle hues and elegant ornaments. The plants were all alive and watered. The shelves were all dusted. The carpet and the curtains were on speaking terms with each other. The lighting was delicate and the bulbs all worked. For Moses, it was like entering an alternative reality.

Moses grabbed another bottle of beer and slouched over to the couch. He'd decided to make a slight effort for the party and was reasonably well turned out in a black shirt and tan slacks. Beside him, Bill scowled in a sweaty green T-shirt and scuffed blue jeans. For once,

Moses felt over-dressed.

"So, Moses," Bill said, tapping his fourth brandy and ginger, "are you heading anywhere after this funeral? Or will you be too busy writing the Ten Commandments?"

"No." Moses shrugged. "I've lost interest in going out since Natalie handed me the elbow."

"She was a hot girl." Bill grinned at Moses. "Great legs! Both of them. I actually saw her in town yesterday evening. She was talking to this guy –"

"Was he a big, long, lanky, bandy-legged, ugly rake of a thing?"

"Well, that's one way of describing him. She seemed to be quite taken with him. They were kissing each other as the sun began to sink lazily in the west. It looked so romantic, it'd make you want to weep. Or puke your ring up."

"Who are you? The wicked messenger? I could do without hearing –"

"Anyway, if Natalie's out of the picture, Moses, what you need to do is cart your carcass off to one of the trendy nightclubs in town. You might meet some young blonde to take your mind off the redhead. It's not that difficult. Even I can score in nightclubs. When the toxic tyrant queen isn't with me, of course."

"Oh really?" Moses sensed another of Bill's fantasies coming on. "I'd say Clinton was president the last time you scored in a nightclub!"

"I was in Roolie Boolie's on Kennedy Street on Wednesday night. After the whole swinger adventure fell apart because you wouldn't co-operate. Remember that?"

"I'm not likely to forget it!"

"I hooked up with this mad one on the dance floor." Bill settled himself more comfortably on the couch, his drink sloshing carelessly in the glass. "She was wearing some loose green outfit and precious little else."

"Did you see any rabbit action?"

"She had an apartment in the suburbs of nowhere. She nearly munched the face off me in the taxi. Then she takes me up to her gaff and practically rips the clothes off me in the kitchen when I'm trying to swallow some headache tablets. My fucking skull was busting."

"And your trousers, I'd imagine." Moses couldn't help getting drawn into Bill's fantasy. "What did she do next?"

"Well, she started baking an apple pie… What the hell do you think she did? She dragged me by the boxers into her bedroom… I nearly died when I saw what she had in there."

"What? A sadomasochism parlour?"

"No…"

"A flock of kinky sheep?"

"No!"

"What then?"

"Her fucking husband!"

"Get away!" Moses stared at Bill. "She had her husband's corpse in her bedroom."

"Who said anything about a corpse?" The Monkees' "I'm A Believer" provided an unlikely backdrop for Bill's story. "He's sitting up in the bed reading a fucking newspaper. I nearly shit a bucket of bricks. I expected him to take a shotgun from under the pillow and shoot the bollocks off me. My only concern was how I was going to explain this to Tiffany when she visited me in the castration ward."

"So what was it? Did you end up in a merry threesome after all?"

"No. That I could handle." Bill shuddered. "It turns out that he liked watching his wife have sex with complete strangers. He wanted to film us!"

"That's… um… innovative."

"It's fucking weird. I wasn't going to be a peep show for anyone. I got the hell out of there."

"You could have ended up on some reality TV show. Or gone viral on YouTube." *Poor Bill. His head is even more screwed up than mine. His fantasies would probably cause the entire Internet to crash in disgust. Even the deep web would think twice before hosting them.* "Anyway, I'm heading outside for a smoke. Get a bit of fresh air."

"You're going out into the fresh air for a smoke? You're obviously comfortable with the contradiction."

"A contradiction is sometimes the best place to be."

Ellington Court was dark and quiet. Moses leaned his back against the wall and lit up his cigarette and inhaled deeply.

I wish I'd filmed myself and Natalie. The tape would come in handy when my memory starts to go…

"Hiya, Moses."

Moses looked down.

Floyd smiled up at him.

The squirrel was wearing blue jeans and an Elvis T-shirt and chewing contentedly on a smouldering cigar.

"Hello, Floyd! How are you keeping?"

"Sound, bud. Just sound. God, that Bill talks an awful mountain of steaming shite, doesn't he? He and Fred would get on like a fertiliser factory on fire. I'd say the only action Bill gets is when Tiffany gives him permission to join her fun."

"Well, at least he has someone."

"You're not going to start wailing about Natalie again, are you? I left my umbrella at home. Face it, she's walked away for good, on those fabulous legs of hers."

"You know, when she used to smile, I could forget everything." Moses threw his cigarette on the ground, watching the sparks explode on the tarmac. "Even if I was on fire or falling off a cliff, her smile could make it all seem right."

"I hate to shatter your illusions." Floyd shook his head sadly, the cigar smoke swirling around his ears. "But there were many times in the past when she smiled and you had absolutely nothing to do with it."

"You really know how to make a guy feel better, Floyd!"

"I'm trying to reacquaint you with an old-fashioned concept called reality, you mangy muppet. You stick with me, bud, and you'll be fine. Remember what I said about Elvis. Throw away the past and reinvent yourself."

"Come back from the dead like Lazarus, perhaps?"

"You don't need to do anything that drastic. You really should stop listening to that daffodil priest! You don't have to accept what you've been given. Don't give up the hunt yet. In fact, I saw a cute little doll going into the party earlier. She didn't have Natalie's legs, but the rest of her looked mighty fine."

"Anyway, Floyd, I'd better head back in." Moses stamped out his still-smouldering cigarette. "Do you want to join the party? I'm sure Lucy wouldn't mind." *She did, after all, tell me to bring along a friend.*

"I'd prefer to stay out here. That music she has on gets on my nuts."

Moses walked back into the building, trying to ignore the sound of the squirrel humming "Return To Sender".

I don't care if it's real, I don't care if it's not,
She's always on my mind and that's all I've got.
My thoughts are heavy, my head is light.
She's stirring your coffee, she's stirring you blood,
Lighting your fire, she's chopping your wood,
But at least there'll be a party in the cemetery tonight.

Party In The Cemetery
Fingers Flaherty

"Moses," Lucy said, taking his hand as he walked back into her apartment. "Would you mind keeping my niece Bubbles company for a while? I need to mingle. She popped by unexpectedly earlier this evening."

"Um… sure… I suppose…"

"Great. You'll like her, Moses."

"Really?" *How do you know what I'll like? I don't even know what I like myself. I hope Lucy isn't trying to set me up with some abandoned pet.* "I'll try to keep her entertained."

"Just don't ask her about her ex-boyfriend." Lucy shuddered. "Or any boyfriends. Or men in general. It's a touchy subject with her.

Anyway, she's getting herself a drink in the kitchen, if you want to go and introduce yourself."

Lucy headed into the sitting room, from where Johnny Hicks's "Hamburger Hop" could be heard playing. Moses took a deep breath and went into the kitchen.

Bubbles was glaring out the window, a glass of wine in her hand. She looked to be about twenty-five, with short curly brown hair. An expensive-looking cream business suit covered her slim figure.

Moses spent some seconds trying to think up of a devastatingly sexy opening line.

"Hi there," he said, giving up. "Are you escaping from the party?"

"Oh hello!" She turned to look at him and smiled. "Finally, someone under ninety has turned up. I just popped by to borrow some books off Lucy and it turns out she's having this party. However, I didn't know anyone and I felt as out of place as a Boney M karaoke machine in a funeral parlour."

Moses opened a bottle of beer.

"My name's Moses. Can I get you more wine?"

"No, I'm fine." She pointed to her half-full glass. "I'll only have one social glass and then I'll head on. If I have too much wine, I'll start swinging from the lights and belting out Gladys Knight classics."

"Really?" *We've got an interesting one here. Better keep Bill away from her!* "Cool! Are you sure you don't want just another bit more?"

"No, thanks. My name's Bubbles."

"Yes, Lucy mentioned –"

"Obviously, it's not my real name, ha ha ha. Any parent who'd christen their daughter Bubbles should be arrested for child abuse. I

119

don't want you thinking I was born in a bucket of washing-up liquid. No, my real name's Angela. One of my ex-boyfriends named me Bubbles because… Well, let's not get into that."

"No, it's probably best that –"

"He wanted to change everything about me, the prick." Bubbles put the glass down on the counter. "He just couldn't accept me as I was. Always had to change things to suit his world view. Bastard! Thank God I'm no longer going out with him. Still, the name stuck. In one way, it's a constant reminder of him. In another way, it's a reminder that I've moved on. I've moved on big time. That bastard can do what he wants now. See if I care. My life's too full to be wasting time thinking about him. You can't waste your time worrying about the past, can you?"

"No." Moses was relieved to finally find an opening in the conversation. "It's always best to move on… But it's not always easy. Sometimes you can find yourself haunted by very persistent ghosts. They can do your head in."

Moses tried to shake the image of Natalie out of his head. She was also drinking a glass of wine, laughing at some joke. Her whole body seem to ripple in mirth. Moses would have happily spent the whole evening gazing at the vision.

"Did you notice that rat on the way in?" Lucy asked. "I'm surprised to see rats in a polished neighbourhood like this."

"That wasn't a rat!" Moses felt compelled to defend Floyd's honour. "That was a squirrel. And a very nice squirrel at that."

"Oh good. I hate rats. They never let you go when they start chewing on you. Like that bastard I was going out with last year. A right rat-faced, two-faced rodent bastard. I'll never forgive that wanker for the way he –"

"You were talking about moving on," Moses reminded her. "We shouldn't let ourselves be haunted by ghosts from the past."

"Whenever I see ghosts from the past," Bubbles continued, without a pause for breath, "I just get out my ghostbuster toolkit and blast them away. You've got to wipe the blackboard clean before you can move on to the next lesson. And if you don't move on to the next lesson, you never learn anything."

In the sitting room, Barry McGuire's "Eve Of Destruction" began ominously rumbling.

"You know," said Moses, as Natalie's image finally faded, "you're right. There comes a time when you must accept that it's time to travel on. Sometimes you have to shake the dust off your shoes and –"

"Not in the kitchen, though. Lucy will kill you." Bubbles exploded into a fit laughing. "Oh Lord, it's always good to see the funny side of things, isn't it? If you didn't take time out to laugh, you'd probably climb up the first bell tower you see and then start shooting people completely at random just to pass the time."

"Um... yeah." Moses took a few subtle steps away from Bubbles. "They say it's easier to smile than –"

"So, is it Moses as in the biblical guy with those two huge stones? How did you end up with a name like that? Did your mother find you in a basket? That'd make you a basket case, ha ha ha ha."

"Well, anyway..." Moses glanced towards the door. It seemed to be seven miles away. "I suppose I should –"

"I talk a lot because I find it cuts down on the amount of bullshit I have to listen to." Bubbles took a contemplative sip of wine. "I learnt that when I was going out with Ivor. He was an arsehole beyond repair. Hopeless case. Talked nothing but shite. So if I kept talking, it shut him up. I suppose you could call it a pre-emptive strike."

"I think I'd call it —"

"I used to love interrupting him." Bubbles smiled into the wine. "Knock him right off his tracks before he could tell me another lie. I knew if I got into an argument with him, we'd have to move to Armageddon before we were finished. So it was best not to listen to him."

"Listening is important, I suppose." *Armageddon would be a breeze compared to this bloody conversation.* "Sometimes we don't even know if we are really listening or just —"

"I suppose none of us know what we're hearing, really." Bubbles looked around the kitchen. "Life's like a box of chocolates. Or maybe a lucky dip. I usually get the piece of broken glass when I dip my hand in."

Jesus, this is like talking to a hair drier.

"You see, it's like Cormac used to say," Bubbles continued. "He's this guy I went out with a few years ago. A pot-bellied fucking bucktooth prick, if you want to know the truth. I hope they roast his hairy Sandra Bullocks in hell for all eternity, the two-timing bastard! Anyway, Cormac said something quite interesting once. One of the few times he wasn't talking shite or lying through his ugly broken brown teeth. Fucker! I was always trying to get him to go to the dentist. I tell you, he was lucky I didn't have a dentist drill on me the night I found him in —"

"What did he used to say?"

"God, I can't remember now. Isn't that funny?"

"Hilarious!"

"It can't have been too important. It was always like that with him. Something looked or sounded good on first impression, but when you analysed it, it was nothing. Ever notice that things that seemed profound on first listen eventually reveal themselves to be utterly meaningless bullshit? Anyway, that's all in the past. We can't keep harping on about such things. I just hope a rabid dog chews his dick off while he's sleeping with that poxy slut from Accounting. You live and you learn. A new lesson every day. I think of life as an adventure story."

"I tend to think of it as a Greek tragedy." Moses finished his beer and grabbed another. "There always seems to be something standing around the corner, waiting to throw shit at you. And there's always a huge crowd in the background just waiting to sing about your misfortune and remind you that –"

"You have to rise above all that shit." Bubbles took a deep breath and smiled. "You see, if you take a little time out, you can get perspective. Whenever someone annoys me, I try not to react immediately. Instead, I take deep breaths and slowly count to ten… Then I consider inserting kitchen utensils into their various bodily orifices."

"God, remind me to never –"

"Anyhoo, listen, Moses, it was great chatting to you." Bubbles drained her glass and left it on the counter. "But I must be heading on. I need to get started on these books this evening or I'll never get the project finished. At least I've no brain-dead cretins in the flat anymore, so I might get some work done without having to murder someone. I'll see you around. And I promise to leave the kitchen utensils at home."

Before Moses could say anything, Bubbles had scooped up the books from the table and was gone out the kitchen door to say goodbye to Lucy.

Moses turned his attention back to the image of Natalie that was again swirling in his head.

She's got them sexy legs, she's got them kinky boots,
She's got that marketable body inside them business suits,
The blouse is loose, the money's tight.
She talks like a hurricane blowin' in your ears,
Her careless whispers can reduce men to tears,
There's going to be a party in the cemetery tonight.

Party In The Cemetery
Fingers Flaherty

While Lucy appeared to be trying to extract some sensible conversation from Bill, Moses joined Jesse and Tiffany over in the corner.

Tiffany sat on a chair beside Jesse. She was wearing black jeans and a light green top. Tiffany was thirty-two years old, with short blonde hair and a full figure. Some days she looked older. This was one of those days.

"So, are you having a good time, Moses?" Tiffany sounded as if her edges of sobriety were beginning to blur. "The place is buzzing! Or is that just my ears acting up again?"

"I think I'll head off now," Jesse said with a smile. "I'm getting too old for these parties."

Moses knew Jesse too well to be offended by his rudeness. Jesse was just looking for an excuse to leave.

"Goodbye, Jesse." Tiffany looked up from her bottle. "Thanks for listening to me. I was probably talking complete and utter shite."

Jesse laughed and walked over to the couch. He tapped Lucy gently on the shoulder.

"Jesse!" She beamed, looking up at him. "How are you?"

"I'm actually going to head on now, Lucy. Thanks for inviting me."

"Are you going?" Her face showed deep disappointment. "Won't you stay just a little bit longer?"

She placed her hand on Jesse's arm and gripped it.

"I'll see you tomorrow, Lucy," he said, his smile lingering.

Moses watched Jesse walk towards the door, wondering if Jesse would ever get what he wanted.

"He's a very strange man," Tiffany remarked to Moses as Jesse walked out the door. "But even he makes more sense than Bill. In fact, he's probably the only man who doesn't talk complete shite in this building... Speaking of which, I suppose I'd better go talk to my boyfriend."

Having been abandoned by three people in the last five minutes, Moses decided it was time to go outside for another smoke. He let the evening chill massage him as he listened to John Lennon's "Instant Karma" waft out from Lucy's apartment.

"What are you doing out here on your own?"

Moses yelped with fright, swallowing a mouthful of smoke.

"Oh, hi, Lucy. I was just having a quiet moment here and... er..."

"Recovering from Bubbles, perhaps?" Lucy laughed. Moses noticed that she sounded slightly tipsy. "I hope she didn't blast your ears off. She has some relationship issues that she really needs to work out."

"No, she was fine. She's a... complex creature. I certainly wouldn't want to get on the wrong side of her. But she has a good philosophy of life, beneath all her psychotic rage. She knows the importance of letting go of the past. There's a lesson in there for me, I suppose."

"Well, just make sure you don't end up like her!" Lucy suddenly frowned. "Do you think Jesse had a good time?"

"I'm sure he did... He didn't say that he didn't anyway."

"Yes." Lucy didn't sound convinced. "He seemed fairly... I don't know... quiet, detached. Even more so than usual! God, I hope he didn't feel obligated to come."

"Listen, if Jesse didn't want to come, no one would have forced him to come. Not even Fingers Flaherty."

"Yes, he can be as immovable as a rock, can't he?"

"Indeed." Moses grinned, his curiosity antenna twitching. "Anyway, I'm sure Jesse would never get angry with you."

"Oh really?" Lucy's eyebrows shot up. "And what gives you that... interesting idea?"

"Well, he seems to be quite... em... er... fond of you." *Oh Christ, Jesse will boil me alive if he finds out what I've said! Shut up before you do any damage.* "In his own odd, detached way, of course."

"Of course." Lucy nodded. "He's a very... deep... er... interesting man... He can be a bit... Anyway, enough of that! I'm sure you don't want to be listening to a lonely woman who's had too much to drink. Thank you for coming to the party. Go back inside and get warm."

Moses walked back in to the sitting room, happy to leave Lucy in peace with her thoughts. The room was quiet, except for John Lennon shining on.

Bill was fast asleep on Tiffany's shoulder, snoring like a busted harmonica, drooling like a drunken baby. Tiffany was looking at him, an indecipherable expression on her face.

"I'll be off now," Moses said.

"What?" Tiffany looked up, confused. "Oh, right! See you, Moses."

"Looks like Bill has had a good night."

"The life and soul of any party! The wheel is still spinning, but the hamster died a long time ago. I suppose I'd better start thinking of waking him up. You don't have a blowtorch handy, by any chance?"

Moses went out into the hall and began walking up the stairs.

Floyd stood at his apartment door, wearing red and white striped pyjamas and a well-pressed paisley dressing gown. On his feet were fluffy black slippers.

"Hiya, Moses," Floyd chirped. "I thought I'd drop by before I took a hammer and hit the sack."

"I like your dressing gown. Very snazzy!"

"What, this old thing?" Floyd gave a small twirl. "It's ancient."

"Do you want to come in for coffee?"

"I can't drink coffee late at night. It keeps me awake for hours. And that's enough to drive any squirrel off its nut. Ha ha ha."

Moses had no idea why the squirrel was laughing.

"That Bill isn't all there up here, if you know what I mean." Floyd tapped his head. "He's so full of shit, he'd be able to fertilise the Phoenix Park."

"God, you're in rare form tonight!"

"You really need to put yourself out in the marketplace again. Go down, Moses. Come down from your whining mountain. Bubbles is right. Wipe the blackboard clean, with kitchen utensils if necessary. You've been alone too long. Soon you'll be the only person who wants to touch you. And you do enough of that already!"

"Jesus Christ! Would you like to get any more personal?"

"Though, as Woody Allen said, it's sex with someone you love."

"Anyway, Floyd," said Moses, determined to break this line of conversation, "I'd better get in. I'm tired."

Moses went into his apartment and closed the door.

He really did need a good night on the town. He'd ring Banjo and head out soon. Paint this city red. That would get his life back on the tracks. Reinvent himself. Be a success in the marketplace.

He hoped.

Call for an ambulance, call for the priest,
My head is locked, my dreams are released,
My shattered heart can't beat, my broken teeth can't bite.
I've learnt my lesson, the price I have to pay,
I'll stay indoors the next time I hear them say
There's gonna be a party in the cemetery tonight.

Party In The Cemetery
Fingers Flaherty

Such A Night

Marie Antoinette Blues

I woke up this morning with my head in a guillotine,
When I woke up this morning, this head was in a guillotine.
At least the view is nice, at least the basket's clean.
Let them eat cake, we've poisoned the bread.

I want to shake things up, I don't want a revolution,
I just want to shake things up, we don't need no revolution.
She's putting on that uniform, she's mixin' that solution.
Let them eat cake, let them starve until they're dead.

Let's go to the jungle, babe, let's go swingin' from the vine,
Let me take you the jungle, babe, we'll swing from the vine.
Let me find my loincloth, let me finish this wine.
Let them eat cake, the sugar's gone to their head.

These women chew me up, and then they spit me out,
These women like to chew me up, they like to spit me out.
Don't say a word, babe. I'm lost in your mouth.
Let them eat cake, the animals have been fed.

I hear distant drums, I hear a native beat,
Is that them distant drums? Is that the native beat?
Give me my war paint, get my dancin' feet.
Let them eat cake, until their eyes go red.

Chapter 7

The White Man Dancing

Throwin' up the whiskey, throwin' up the gin,
Throwin' up the vodka, throw it all back in.
White man will be runnin' when I got the white man's gun,
White man will be dancin' for his supper when I'm done.
He's got the white man dancin' blues.

White Man Dancin' Blues
Fingers Flaherty

Moses kept his eyes on his reflection in the mirror, gently guiding the razor across the shaving foam on his chin. For some seconds, the only sound in the bathroom was the scrape of the blade against the stubble.

Floyd started pacing up and down the bath. It being casual Friday, he was dressed in white sandals, red shorts and a blue Hawaiian T-shirt.

Moses splashed warm water on his face to rinse off the shaving foam residue. He dried himself, wincing as the rough towel scratched against his raw skin. However, looking at his reflection, he felt the result was worth the pain.

"You missed a bit," Floyd declared.

"Where?" Moses squinted into the steamed-up mirror. "No, I didn't."

"Yes, you did. There's a small hairy patch below your chin."

"That's deliberate," Moses lied. "It's the in look."

Moses splashed on his aftershave, trying to ignore the sound of the squirrel whistling "Suspicious Minds".

Floyd's nose twitched as he sniffed loudly.

"God almighty, Moses! You're laying on the aftershave a bit thick. You're making my eyes water."

"I'm not going to take advice on personal hygiene from a squirrel who's wearing a Hawaiian shirt. I'm just trying to make myself beautiful."

"I don't think you're going to find a plastic surgeon working this late in the evening. You'll smell like you're in heat! So is this your Elvis reinvention? Are you going to slip into a jumpsuit and sweat a waterfall?"

"Leave me alone!" Moses sprayed on deodorant. "I'm just pressing on and trying to have a good night."

"I know what you're thinking, Moses. No matter what you do at work, you'll never prove your manhood to Fred now. So you have to move the game to a different arena. If you can tell Fred that you pulled a flock of chicks in some nightclub, you'll prove your masculinity to him. Then you'll no longer feel inadequate at work. Your logic is as subtle as your aftershave."

Moses took his shirt off the door rack. It was his grey shirt with black buttons, one of the few shirts that fit him comfortably.

"Why on earth are you wearing that undertaker's shirt?" Floyd asked, his face scrunching into a whiskery furrow.

"It's my lucky shirt!"

"Maybe you'll get lucky tonight and meet Bubbles again!" Floyd started laughing. "She'd be the right tonic for you. I love a fiery girl!"

"Well, go marry an arsonist then!" Moses scrutinised his reflection in the mirror. His confidence was dwindling by the second. "Listen, Floyd, I'm nearly ready to head, so... go away. I'll probably see you tomorrow."

Moses opened the bathroom window and Floyd scrambled out. After slamming the window shut, Moses went down to his bedroom. He grabbed his brown suede jacket from the wardrobe.

Time to put myself back in the marketplace!

Before he got to the marketplace, however, he bumped into Lucy in the Ellington car park.

"Hi, Moses! Are you going to a funeral?"

"What? No! I'm going out clubbing!"

"Oh!" Lucy looked lost for words. "Well, the good girls don't judge boys by appearance, I suppose."

"I just need a night on the town," Moses explained, while contemplating returning to his apartment for a complete costume change. "It's been another farcical week at work Some days I'm terrified I'll be fired, and some days I'm terrified I won't be."

"Work is only a small part of your life," Lucy replied, with a smile. "You should focus on the other parts.... Which reminds me, Bubbles was asking for you today."

"Oh, really?" *Oh, Christ!* "That's... um... How is she?"

"She's just great. She really enjoyed meeting you at the party last week. In fact, between me and you, I think she'd like to meet you again."

"I'm sure that'd be —"

"She's coming over to me later this evening. If you wait a while, the two of you could go clubbing together."

"Well, the thing is…" Moses vainly tried to keep the panic out of his voice. "I told Banjo I'd meet him and take him on the town. He's struggling with his joke of a thesis as much as I'm struggling with my joke of a job. And… well… Anyway, I'll see you soon, Lucy."

Moses couldn't help noticing that Lucy was laughing as he ran out of the car park.

White wine, red wine, peach schnapps and lemon tea,
Whiskey and cola, vodka and lime. What colour will my vomit be?
Did you never realise that I'd move in for the kill?
That you'll be dancin' to my tune until you pay your bill?
Sweatin' away with the white man dancin' blues.

White Man Dancin' Blues
Fingers Flaherty

Banjo was already well on the road to alcohol-induced oblivion.

He wasn't falling all over the place. He wasn't drooling or muttering to himself. He wasn't even vomiting on the floor or dancing the Lambada with a chair leg.

But there was a determination in the way he was drinking that pointed to only one blurry destination.

Banjo had the warrior gear on. He looked relatively clean-shaven. His long black hair seemed to have been washed at least once in the previous fortnight. He was wearing his short-sleeved black-and-yellow striped shirt; he explained that it was his "lucky wasp" and he never failed to sting when he wore it. And he was wearing what looked like a brand-new pair of white khakis.

The night was progressing along nicely so far. The crowd in The Merry Monk was young and noisy. Although it was still only 10.00, quite a few were already thoroughly lashed, dancing to Catty's "Vomit Morning".

Banjo's eyes were eagerly drinking up the scene, ricocheting from wall to wall. His fingers twitched excitedly, always a sign that he was going into heat.

"Take it steady." Moses laughed. "The night is still young."

"No harm in being the early bird."

"Yeah, but you might end up like the early worm!"

Moses glanced around the pub. Most of the people were in their twenties, drinking bottles of beer or spirit mixers. Smartphones chirped to one another in shrill mating calls. The carpet of shouted conversation smothered the room.

Moses had moved on to gin and tonics, trying to erase the memory of Bubbles from his mind. Banjo was on straight whiskey and crooked grins.

The women all were good looking, wearing Friday-night best. Moses searched in vain for one who would set his spark smouldering. But everywhere he looked, he saw shadows of Natalie. A small woman with black, gelled hair and tanned skin surveyed the room through cow-brown eyes, eyes just like Natalie's. A woman in a short green skirt and white boots had Natalie's tentative smile. A sultry woman in a tight blue dress had short ginger hair, just like Natalie.

Moses sighed as Anthony's Freshman's "The Ghost of Our Love" started playing. The spark was as dark as ever.

"What the hell's wrong with you?" Banjo asked, looking at Moses. "You look like you've woken up at the wrong funeral."

"I'm thinking of setting up an online dating service," Moses answered. "Get into the social media game, like Fred told us. Help people find their matches in the cloud. Because there's fuck all chance of finding a match down here!"

"Jesus, that'd be like Prince Philip setting up a diplomacy course." Banjo laughed. "I mean, you haven't exactly had much luck in that department lately!"

"That's why it's a good idea." The tonic fizz tickled Moses's gums. "People think they know what they want. You see, when someone describes his ideal woman, you should set him up with the exact opposite. Because that's the one you always fall for, the exact opposite of your ideal, the person you least expect to turn you on. It always hits you like an invisible truck."

The woman in the tight blue dress was glaring at some guy who was talking to her. His left hand clutched her shoulder, his other clutched a bottle of Miller. He had the desperate, smiling expression of someone trying to explain why he had been found handcuffed to a gerbil in a brothel. Blue Dress was looking at him through new eyes and not liking what she saw.

"You always are struck by people who remind you of your ideal," said Moses, rummaging in his jeans pocket for his cigarettes. "But when you look closely, you realise they are only a shadow. You're drawn to the flickering shadow because you think it will lead you to the flame. But then her nose isn't right. The eyes look the wrong way. Her laugh is too loud. There are too many teeth in her mouth. All you can see are the flaws."

"Are you pissed already?"

"It's the ones who don't remind you of the ideal who never disappoint." Moses rummaged in his other pocket, still not finding the cigarettes. "The ones who remind you of nobody."

"Are you having a wank, Moses? You've been burrowing in your pocket for the last minute. Couldn't you slip into the jacks and be a bit more discreet? Wanking in public is considered bad form nowadays, even in this place."

"I'm looking for my cigarettes."

"They're in your undertaker shirt pocket, you tool."

"So they are," said Moses, looking down. "I don't remember putting them there."

"You were probably too busy talking bullshit to notice."

The woman in the green skirt was talking to two stocky, rugby-type guys in muscle-defined white T-shirts as Bladder's "Lost in Love" began playing. Both had army haircuts beneath their battered baseball caps. Her slightly unfocused eyes fluttered from one T-shirt to the other, as if trying to decide. The guys were eyeing her up and down, left and right, but were also taking backup glances at any other women who walked by.

"It's the one who reminds you of no one who will knock you over a cliff." Moses blinked his eyes to steady his vision. His eyelashes got tangled together in the struggle. "That will be the philosophy behind my dot com."

"Complete bullshit!" Banjo was staring at a skinny girl in a red business suit. She was standing alone at the bar, waiting to be served.

She gazed at her reflection in the bar mirror. "Everyone reminds you of someone. That's how you remember people."

"Who do I remind you of?" Moses immediately suspected that he'd regret the question.

"Jingles," said Banjo, not taking his eyes off the red suit.

"Who the hell is Jingles?"

"This little Yorkshire terrier I had when I was a boy."

"I remind you of a Yorkshire terrier?"

"Yeah." Banjo turned to Moses and broke out in a grin. "You really do, actually. He was a whinging little bastard who was always yelping for attention. And if you yelled at him, he'd shit on the carpet just to spite you."

"When did I last shit on your carpet?"

"You know what I mean." Banjo laughed, glancing back to the red suit at the bar. "You can't cope with any setbacks. Your chin scrapes off the pavement and you let out despairing sighs that could power a windmill. Jingles used to do the same."

Moses turned his attention back to the crowd. He was just in time to see the woman in the blue dress storm off to the tune of Hoodlum's "Switchblades and Caviar". Her boyfriend gaped after her, dumbfounded, his half-empty bottle of Miller dangling precariously from his fingers.

"Look, Moses, I'm going to scoot over to the bar and try my luck with… That chick in the red suit looks like she might be on for it. Do you want a drink?"

"Get me another gin and tonic."

"Cool," said Banjo, heading off to the bar. "Wish me luck."

Moses watched Banjo strut over to Red Suit. The woman in the green skirt was kissing one of the rugby guys. The other guy stood beside them, dumbly, not knowing what to do with his muscles. He cast forlorn looks at every female within glancing distance.

The small woman with the black, gelled hair was on a girls' night out. She sat with four others at a table. The other women were laughing and gasping and wheezing loudly. Gelled Hair looked bored. Her eyes had a vacant stare when she smiled, not registering what she was supposed to be smiling about. Cow-brown eyes. Just like Natalie.

Red Suit was checking her watch incessantly while Banjo tried to work his charm on her. He was leaning against the bar, grinning down on her. She gazed coldly back up at him.

Moses suddenly noticed a woman wearing a pink blouse and black pants. She was fingering an unlit cigarette. Moses squinted his eyes to see her through the haze that seemed to envelop her.

Natalie never wore pink. She thought it was too garish. And Natalie was left-handed. This woman held the cigarette in her right hand.

The woman noticed him staring at her. Her eyes froze for a second. Green eyes, Moses noticed. Then she smiled.

Sara Zuma's "Rainfall at Midnight" was now playing. The woman ambled cautiously towards Moses. Nervously. Not at all like Natalie's aggressive stride.

Moses grinned at her, his heart thumping.

Dear God, don't let me mess this up!

The woman was beside him now.

"Sorry, but I couldn't get a light off you, could I?" She smiled, holding up her cigarette.

"Sure." Moses plucked the lighter from his shirt pocket with a cool flourish. His packet of cigarettes shot out too and struck him on the chin. "Ouch! Shit!"

The woman laughed. Moses smiled back, ruefully rubbing his chin. *Bastard cigarettes!*

They went outside to smoke. He held the lighter out and flicked on the flame.

She bent her face towards his hand and lit her cigarette. The flame flickered in her face, making her green eyes twinkle.

"Thanks," she said, exhaling a puff of smoke.

She had a northern accent. Natalie was from Cork. Moses's heart beat faster.

"So," Moses said, praying that he wasn't about to wreck his chances, "are you enjoying the night?"

"It's going pretty good. And you?"

"Yeah, cool. I like this place."

"It's pretty crowded, though." She shrugged. "As per."

Moses froze, his heartbeat stopping for a second.

Ah shit!

That was Natalie's phrase. Whenever she complained about anything, she always ended it by saying "As per". One morning, when he was in a werewolf hangover, all hairy and growling, he lost patience with her when she said it for the fourth time. "As per bloody what?" he'd shouted. Natalie gave him the glaring silent treatment for the rest of the day after that.

Moses exchanged small talk with the woman for a while. Her name was Nora. She was a computer programmer. She was just back from a holiday in New Orleans. She'd had a great time.

Moses decided to bring the wasted charade to an end.

"Sorry, Nora, but I see my friend in there looking kinda lost. As… usual. I'll catch you later."

"Fine." She sighed, stubbing out her cigarette.

Moses walked over to Banjo, feeling wretched. Banjo was still trying to work his charm on Red Suit.

"This is my friend Moses," Banjo said to Red Suit, when Moses tapped him on the shoulder. "He's got a great sense of humour."

"He must have," Red Suit said, "if he's friends with you."

"Tell her a joke, Moses."

"Um… right." *Thanks for putting me on the spot, Banjo!* "How about this? This horse walks into a bar. The barman says, 'Why the long face?' Ha ha ha."

Red Suit scrutinised Moses as if he were an alien microbe.

"Inside you're laughing, aren't you?" Moses said to her.

"Inside I'm explaining to the judge why I stabbed you," she replied.

"I can beat that," declared Banjo. "This giraffe walks into a bar. The barman says, 'You've got some neck showing your face around here!' God, I'm so on a roll, you could call me 'Butter'!"

"That's not that I want to call you," Red Suit said.

"Try this one then," Moses said, deciding he had no more self-respect to lose. "This monkey walks into a bar. The monkey says 'Ouch!' It's an iron bar."

"I've got one for you," Red Suit replied, finishing her drink.

"These two drunken dickheads walk into a bar. Every girl in the place jumps into the taxi to the airport and flies out of the country. Goodbye!"

Before Moses or Banjo could say anything, Red Suit had disappeared into the crowd.

"Come on!" Moses picked up his gin and tonic and poured it down his throat. "Let's head to Zebra's."

"Yeah. This place is dead. You'd get more action if you were buried alive in the Mojave Desert. Talk about being unlucky. I think I was born under a bad sign."

"You were born under a cabbage patch!"

They ploughed their way through the drunken crowd as Mumble's "Break into the Jail" played from the speakers.

Every touch feels like it comes from outer space, every breath gets lost in my throat,
Every picture looks like it was done by Picasso, the menu is something that James Joyce wrote.
Tomorrow mornin' gonna strap white man to the plough,
White man gonna learn who the master is now.
He'll have the white man dancin' blues.

White Man Dancin' Blues
Fingers Flaherty

Two hours later, Moses and Banjo were stumbling along Robinson Street, glowering at the pavement.

"Well, that was a complete bust!" Banjo kicked an empty beer can down the street. "What the hell were we thinking? Zebra's is always a disaster. Well, either it's fantastic or a complete waste of time. Black or white. But it looked like we might have got some action there. I think we were well in with those two nurses. Especially that young one who looked like a cross between Judy Garland and an ostrich. Of course, you ruined our chances by looking as bored as a lion in a vegetable shop."

"Banjo, they were lesbians. I thought you –"

"Oh, come on, Moses." Banjo snorted. "That's a fairly pathetic excuse. Just because we didn't score with them doesn't mean –"

"They were kissing each other, you stupid jalopy!"

"Oh…" Two blue, bleary orbs of complete incomprehension gaped at Moses. "I thought they were just having an intimate conversation. Maybe they were whispering about us. Trying to decide which one of us –"

"They were giving each other tongue. Now let's call it a night."

"No. There's one more place we can try. We're near Derek Street. Let's go to Halogen."

Moses took a deep breath and followed the staggering figure towards Derek Street. He threw his eyes up to the sky. The stars were hopelessly faded. The moon shimmered, thrashing against invisible clouds. Moses decided that he wouldn't drink any more alcohol tonight.

The Halogen bouncers sourly eyed them up before they nodded them in.

As they handed over the money for their tickets, Moses was already beginning to regret not going straight home. The possibility of meeting Bubbles didn't seem to be the worst option anymore. A wall of heat and noise hit them when they reached the dance floor. The place was crowded and mists of perspiration fluttered towards the ceiling.

The Razor Blades' latest industrial dance hit, "Diggin' Elvis", blared across the sweaty room. The DJ had remixed the song beyond recognition, turning an up-tempo piece of disco fluff into a sledgehammer barrage of riffs and relentless rhythms. The strobe lights created a dizzy, almost hysterical, atmosphere. The people on the dance floor were gyrating in a trance-like frenzy.

The walls were daubed nightmare-inducing red and grey. The purple tiles were slippery with spilled wine and sweat. Moses tried to make eye contact with some of the women on the dance floor but the dancers either had their eyes closed tight or wide open in glassy stares of oblivion.

The drug dealers have been doing a brisk trade in the toilets tonight.

Banjo turned and said something, but Moses couldn't hear him because some frantic drum and synthesiser orgy was now bellowing from the speakers.

"What did you say?" he yelled.

"I said," roared Banjo into Moses's ear, causing him to wince, "that this is a great place. Look at all that skin-tight talent grinding it out on the dance floor."

"It's a dump! What the hell possessed you to come here?"

"Just relax and get into the buzz! This is one of the best joints in Dublin. I hear that Bono and Colin Farrell have often been seen here."

"I don't care if Eamon de Valera and Saint Patrick have been seen here. I'm never setting foot in this corner of hell again!"

"What you need is a bottle of wine and some eager young thing on your lap to get your blood pumping again."

Banjo screamed his order at the barman as a jungle choir began chanting above the synthesisers.

After some minutes, they grabbed their bottle of wine and went over to an empty table at the back of the room. The table was in the chill-out area. Air conditioners hummed at full blast and, through some magic acoustic engineering, the music sounded muffled here. The lights were dimmed, creating an intimate atmosphere. Someone had scribbled "Welcome to the Erection Section" on the back wall.

"Some place alright," said Banjo. "Get a dose of that silver one dancing in the corner. She's some space-age chick and a half, no question. Ooooh-eeeeee, ride me high, yeah!"

Moses gripped the edge of the table and squinted to focus his eyes.

Just when I thought this fucking bust of a night couldn't get any worse!

Rita, the Space Invader from Murphy's bar, was lost in a trance on the dancefloor. She was wearing a skin-tight silverish dress and knee-high grey boots. Specks of silver glitter sparkled in her blonde hair. She was dancing enthusiastically, with her arms, legs and body thrusting rhythmically to the monotonous crunch of the music.

However, it was her friend who caught Moses's attention. She was wearing a loose red dress that wrapped itself effortlessly around her slim, swaying body. Her white shoes bounced on the dance floor. She was using her hand to brush her wavy black hair back out of her face. Her eyes were closed in the rapture of the dance, her lips slowly mouthing the inane lyrics of the song.

"I'll see if they'll join us," said Banjo, suddenly stumbling up from the couch. Before Moses could say anything, Banjo was shimmying over to the two women.

Moses didn't have the energy to start dancing to music that he loathed, so he slouched back in the couch and gulped a hefty mouthful of wine.

Moses smiled as he watched Banjo on the dance floor. Banjo had somehow bulldozed his way over to the two women and he was now shakily strutting himself. Red Dress was still locked in her own rhythmic trance, but Rita raised interested eyebrows in Banjo's direction. They were soon shouting small talk at each other as their bodies unsuccessfully tried to co-ordinate into some mutual groove.

The song finally ended and, to Moses's amazement, Banjo brought the two girls back to the table. He looked wrecked from his exertions.

"Moses," Banjo declared, between sweaty gasps of breath, "this is Rita and Saoirse. Saoirse, Rita, this miserable terrier is Moses."

Rita's glittered eyebrows twitched when she saw Moses.

"Oh, God!" She sighed. "Not you again."

"Do you know this reject?" Banjo asked, leaning in to Rita's ears.

"We've met a few times. I never forget an ugly face. And by the way, please stop nibbling my earlobe. I'm not a Twizzler!"

"Hello." Moses barely looked at Rita. "Fancy seeing you again."

"Do you remember I told you about my flatmate? Well, this is Saoirse, the freedom-loving girl who likes charity cases. I'm sure you'll get on like a house on fire."

Moses was wishing the nightclub would catch fire as Saoirse collapsed into a paroxysm of giggling, her red dress practically fluttering in the commotion.

Rita and Saoirse sat on the chairs on the other side of the table.

"I'll get us another bottle of wine," said Banjo, carefully untangling his tongue from Rita's ear, "seeing as this alcoholic here has finished the first one already."

Moses looked at the wine bottle and saw with a shock that Banjo was right. He again decided that he would drink absolutely no more alcohol this night.

"Er... so..." started Moses, trying to keep communication open while Banjo went to the bar, "how are you... um... enjoying the... eh... night?"

Rita looked at him as if he were on day release from the local asylum. Saoirse exploded into another fit of giggling.

"It's okay, I suppose," said Rita, eventually. "It's... whatever... cool."

"I'm not too pushed on it myself."

"Of course you're not. You don't look the type."

Ouch! Bitch!

Moses decided to concentrate on Saoirse instead. She seemed to have recovered from her giggle fit.

"So... em," he said, clearing his throat, "what do you do with yourself?"

"I'm... at college." Saoirse seemed to be making a supreme effort to give him a serious answer. "I'm doing a post-grad course in Trinity on post-colonial theory... Yeah... Cool..."

Great! A stoned intellectual and a sarcastic wagon wrapped in tin foil.

"So what do you do... ahem... with yourself?" asked Saoirse, apparently realising how sharp her answer had sounded.

I work for the poxy Aztech computer company, writing stupid blurbs for products that are so bad they should be banned. My boss is an unhinged psycho shitweed. I spend my day writing lies to sell rubbish to fools. I have become what I used to hate. I am a spiritless, cash-fed office slave.

"I… um… work in marketing."

"Oh." Saoirse seemed to be trying not to laugh in his face. "Right."

Banjo suddenly arrived back holding a bottle of red in one hand and a bottle of white in the other. A wine glass was held precariously under each armpit. He sat on the couch beside Moses and filled the glasses.

The wine was consumed with nervous thirst. Moses silently prayed that the wine was poisoned.

Without warning, Banjo and Rita were all over each other. Her fingers frantically fumbled through his hair as she kissed him hard. Banjo was caught off guard and nearly spilled his glass over Moses.

"Er… you know…" said Saoirse to Moses, looking in disbelief at Rita, "like… how come you weren't out on the dance floor?"

"I don't care for this kind of music," he answered, taking his eyes off the show on the couch. "I hate it. I hate this whole scene. There's something depressing about stoning your brains out and spending hours listening to white noise blaring in a dingy sweat pit."

"Don't be so tight! It's not all bad. Sure, the music's crap, but you have to let yourself go every now and then. Pop some whatevers and swing with the swing."

"This is nothing but drug music. It's marketed towards losers who have lost all meaning in their life. Knock back some pills and listen to electronic rubbish and your life will be better. Give me a break!"

Did I tell you that I'm the youngest old fogie in Dublin?

"So tell me about the course you're doing in Trinity," Moses said.

"It's really interesting," she answered, staring straight into his eyes, seemingly afraid to look at the X-rated movie being rehearsed on the couch in front of her. "I'm specialising in how the white crusade to civilise native tribes failed because it was based on incorrect premises. Dear God, I can't believe that I am talking about this in Halogen!"

"No, go on," urged Moses. She was leaning forward towards him now, her arms spread out on the table in front of her, the curve of her breasts becoming more pronounced. Her knees gently hit his under the table and rested there. "Tell me more."

"Well, you see, the whites thought native cultures were inherently inferior and so they tried to, as they saw it, civilise them, make them more like white culture. God, would you listen to me, what do I sound like? Ha ha ha. Whites were seeing in the natives all the passions that they had denied themselves."

The table rocked suddenly as Banjo's thigh banged against it. Rita let out a giggle. Saoirse frantically gulped her wine, staring straight at Moses.

"How did they… er… fail, then?" asked Moses, staring back at Saoirse just as intently.

"Some 'went native', giving into the native culture. They joined the tribal rituals and danced to the so-called evil rhythms of the jungle. That's why I'm calling my thesis *The White Man Dancing*."

Moses adjusted his legs into a more comfortable position. The wine splashed as he lifted his glass with a trembling hand. He glanced to his side. Rita was now nibbling Banjo's ear. Banjo's hands had disappeared into the folds of her dress. They were both flushed and sweating.

Moses looked at Saoirse and felt a static charge between them, the tingle that makes lovers want to run naked through snow-covered forests in the shimmering moonlight. Or just jump into the nearest taxi back home.

Suddenly, a new song cranked up on the dance floor. Moses could hear a frantic drum beat and a mad brass section kicking into life. An electric bass line began thumping.

"God, I love this song," Saoirse yelled, leaping up. "Come on, let's dance."

Moses sat back on the couch and watched her strike into a wild dance groove, her hair and dress swaying freely all around her.

Beside him on the couch, the action seemed to have cooled down somewhat. Rita was gently stroking Banjo's hair. He was staring down into her eyes, a bedroom smile dripping on his lips.

Moses finished off his wine and stood up. He walked unsteadily towards the dance floor.

"See you in a bit," he shouted back to Banjo.

When he got to the dance floor, the noise was deafening. Everything was shimmering, losing focus. He saw Saoirse and staggered over to her.

"Hi, again," he shouted in her ear.

She opened her eyes and turned to him. She smiled in surprise.

"I thought you didn't dance."

"I don't," he laughed, as he tried to lock into the rhythm, "as you'll shortly discover."

"Just go native!"

He closed his eyes and began dancing. He knew he was making a fool of himself but he didn't care anymore. He began swaying in time to the drum and bass.

The room began to go completely out of focus. The strobe lights kicked in and everything became hallucinogenic. All he could see was Saoirse, dancing before him in a red dress, holding him. The smile continued to play on her moist lips. She was moving closer and closer to him.

The music seemed to get louder. Their bodies pressed against each other, heaving against each other. Their eyes zoomed in closer, almost colliding. Their arms wrapped tighter. He could feel the warmth of the wine on her breath.

The rhythm became more focused.

Their lips touched… and then pressed firmly together.

An electric guitar began screaming.

Moses closed his eyes and completely surrendered to the dance of the tribal rhythm.

Give me a Sunday morning goddess, give me a Saturday night whore,
Give me a mistress with a mattress, give me a nun with a mind like a sewer.
Give me a dancer waving wild and free,
Give me a woman who wants to have fun with me.
I've got the white man dancin' blues.

White Man Dancin' Blues
Fingers Flaherty

Moses yawned and slowly peeled back his eyelids.

Huge green hills rolled away in all directions. The sky pressed down on him, blue and vast, a blanket hiding him from the world. All around him, lush, green sun-soaked fields splashed against the horizon.

Beneath him, the grass felt warm and soft, the gentle blades adjusting themselves to his shape, lightly caressing him.

He realised that he was naked. Sun splashed over his chest. He smiled, feeling the sun tickle across his lips and trickle into his mouth.

Saoirse lay curled up naked beside him, her head resting on his shoulder, her arm thrown across his chest, her breasts heaving gently against his side.

Lambs began to run across the field, shaking the sleep out of their wool, calling to each other, excitedly. Field mice enthusiastically scurried about their business, disturbing no one. A fox rolled in the grass, yawning, content to lie there forever.

A white rabbit hopped towards Moses, a smile on its face. It wanted to tell him something.

Moses turned to the white rabbit, eyes open expectantly.

The rabbit whispered something in Moses's ear.

"Hey, gobshite! Wake the fuck up! I haven't got all bollocksing night, you know!"

Moses jumped back, startled. The blue blanket collapsed.

The cloakroom attendant glared at him. He wore a black Iron Maiden T-shirt over a beer belly. His face was unshaven and severe, under greying crew-cut hair.

Moses couldn't imagine any man looking less like a fluffy white rabbit.

In the background, Cryptoid's "Fields Of Sweat" thumped furiously.

"Where's your fucking ticket, dickhead?" the cloakroom attendant bellowed, shaking Moses's shoulder.

"Here." Moses rubbed the spittle from his face as he handed over the ticket. "Sorry."

"Standing there like a spare prick for the last minute, you were," the attendant grumbled, searching through the racks for Moses's coat. "Don't know what fucking drugs you're on but you need to lay off them. Stick to cough sweets and do us all a bloody favour. Where's this fucking coat?"

"It's a brown suede –"

"I don't give a fuck what it looks like! I'll find it with this sodding ticket. Could be a pink plastic shroud for all I care."

Moses glanced around him, realising that further conversation with the rabbit would be dangerous.

"You kind of drifted off there, Moses." Saoirse smiled at him. "I thought you'd fallen into a coma."

"Oh, I was just thinking of… something." Moses shrugged. "I shouldn't have drunk so much –"

"Here, arsehole," the attendant grunted, flinging the suede jacket at Moses. "Now fuck off back to the asylum."

"Come on," Saoirse said, heading up the stairs.

Moses followed her.

Lead me through the smokin' streets, baby, make sure you don't lose me in the dark.
I stumbled on in blindness guided by your spark.

Should I fall on my sword? Will you hand it to me?
Is it time for me to climb out of the tree?
Where are the white man dancin' blues?

White Man Dancin' Blues
Fingers Flaherty

The air outside Halogen felt cool and crisp. Moses zipped up his jacket and dug his hands into his pockets.

"Let's get something to eat," said Saoirse, grabbing his arm. "I know a late-night cafe on Flaherty Street. You seem to be shivering, Moses."

"I'm just cooling down. It was like a sweat factory in that place."

"Yes, it did get quite hot." Saoirse smiled, squeezing his arm.

"Um… yeah." Moses knew that there was a devastatingly witty response to that somewhere. "It… em… did."

Derek Street was crowding up as the nightclubs began ejecting their clients. Numerous people stumbled blindly in the chilly air, totally lost to their surroundings. Some were vomiting over the railings, groaning loudly. Exhausted students lay on steps, snoring loudly as their friends tried to shake or kick them awake. Some men shouted at each other, throwing drunken punches.

Moses and Saoirse pushed their way through the crowd. Later on, the crowd thinned out when they got to Wolfhound Road. A well-lit street, a few people walking along, steadily, silently.

"Tell me," said Moses, as they moved on to McCarthy Street, "what were you thinking about when we were on the dance floor?"

"I was imagining we were in a jungle, dancing to the tribal dance.

There were bonfires all around us. The natives were playing wild music and sacrificing animals… Maybe I shouldn't have smoked so much wacky backy this evening."

"Oh, I don't know. It doesn't seem to have done you any harm. Not yet, anyway."

"I'll let you know when it starts to… affect my brain," Saoirse said, speaking in an exaggeratedly slow voice. "And then… I'll let you know when… it starts to affect my… brain."

They walked in silence for some minutes, their footsteps echoing in the chilly air.

"And you?" Saoirse said suddenly.

"What about me?"

"What were you thinking about on the dance floor? Advertising slogans? Core markets? Trending paradigms?"

"I was imagining that we were dancing in a palace, actually. There was an orchestra and a giant dance floor. Champagne flowed like… like… something that flows easily…"

"Dear God, what were you on tonight? Tell me more."

The palace ballroom had white marble pillars. Red velvet curtains covered the windows. A huge fire roared in the hearth, its flames throwing dancing shadows flickering on the walls. Outside the plague raged. We had only this one last night. The entire world would die in the morning.

I was in a black evening suit. You wore a red ball gown and white gloves. We gazed into each other's eyes as we danced. The orchestra was playing Vivaldi's "Spring". The members of the orchestra all wore red hooded capes and silver death masks.

And it felt like the springtime of my life! Your hand gripped my waist. I had awoken from a long, dark hibernation. As your lips brushed against my face, everything seemed to make sense.

The moon crawled out from behind the plague-infested clouds. It shimmered through a skylight in the ceiling. A single moonbeam shone on you as the world revolved around us.

"It's far too complex to explain," Moses said. "Maybe some other time."

"We're near Flaherty Street now."

"Good." The king's feast on the palace tables made Moses very hungry. "I need something to soak up the alcohol."

A few late-night cafes stayed open in this part of the city. A lot of people were out and about, and some were probably out of it. A few people stumbled. One or two fell completely. In general, though, people seemed relatively sober, compared to the barbarians on Derek Street. Moses wondered how drunk he looked. He was glad Saoirse was still holding on to his arm.

Then he froze.

"What's up?" asked Saoirse.

Stephen and Krystal were approaching them. They were deep in conversation and hadn't noticed Moses. Krystal was in a brown business suit. Stephen was in casual-Friday white khakis, with a red T-shirt and a tan leather jacket. He looked to be drunk, his face flushed and his hair tangled carelessly.

"It's my brother," Moses whispered. "I don't want to talk to him. He's a bit of a… wanker."

"We could cross the street to avoid him."

"Yes. Let's do… ah, shit!"

Krystal smiled when she saw Moses. She nudged Stephen, who looked up. His bleary eyes widened.

"Hi, Moses," Krystal said. "How are you?"

"Um… er… fine," Moses mumbled. "And you?"

"Just great. We've been to a work party with Stephen's company. He's had a bit too much to drink, as you can probably see."

"Hello, Moses," Stephen muttered, barely audible. "Are you keeping well?"

"Fine," Moses said flatly. "Smashing. Super."

They looked at each other in silence for some seconds. Then Krystal broke out laughing.

"Really, Moses!" Krystal laughed. "Are you not going to introduce us to your friend?"

Moses looked at Saoirse. She smiled back at him. He had almost forgotten she was there.

"Oh yeah," he said. "Stephen, Krystal, this is Saoirse. Saoirse, Stephen and Krystal."

Hands were shaken and greetings exchanged. The awkward silence crept back in.

"So," said Krystal, "where have you been this evening?"

"Halogen," said Saoirse. "We're just on our way from there."

"Really?" Stephen was grinning. "Are you turning into a raver, Moses, on top of everything else?"

Moses glared at Stephen.

"It's a good place sometimes." Saoirse smiled at Moses. "You never know who or what you are going to meet there."

"I see." Krystal's tone indicated that she had worked out the situation. "Sounds like you've had a good night."

"Yes, we have." Moses stared directly at Stephen. "It's been a real good night."

Moses thought he could see jealousy uncoil in Stephen's eyes. Stephen didn't look like he'd had a good night. Moses was curious. He wanted to explore this thread of conversation further, to find out just how bad Stephen's night had been.

"So, Stephen –"

"I was talking to Dad last night," Stephen said suddenly. "He was asking about you."

"Really?" Moses felt the thread snap out of his fingers. Saoirse and Krystal were exchanging small talk. He was stuck with Stephen. "That's… nice."

"He was saying that you've started to get your act together at work. Is that so?"

"Yeah, I suppose." Moses couldn't remember what lies he had said to his father earlier that week. "It's going… well."

"Good." Stephen nodded. "You've got brains and ability, Moses. It's just that you tend to keep them well hidden most of the time."

Moses frowned. This was the closest Stephen had ever come to paying him a compliment. It was a barbed compliment, but it was more than he expected. Maybe it was the drink, maybe it was the cool air, maybe it was Saoirse, but he felt his attitude to Stephen very slightly thaw for the first time in years.

Jesus, this is almost embarrassing.

"Yes," Moses mumbled. "Things are going well. I don't ask for much from life. And that's what I tend to get."

"Well, don't let it get you down. It's not worth it. And let Dad know you're back on the rails. He worries about you."

They stared at each other. Stephen was obviously much drunker than Moses realised, or he would never have said those things. Moses knew that if he spoke to Stephen in the harsh sober light of day tomorrow, Stephen would be as cold and nasty to him as ever. This conversation was nothing more than a tiny blip on a steady chart.

But Moses was glad of the blip.

"Well, there you go," Moses said, shrugging again, totally lost for words.

"Yeah." Stephen nodded, slipping his gruff mask on again.

Saoirse and Krystal seemed to have also hit a conversational roadblock. It was time to escape.

"Well," said Moses, sliding his hand into Saoirse's, "we'll let you go. We don't want to keep you back."

"I'm sure we'll bump into each other again soon, Moses." Krystal smiled. "Hope to meet you again, Saoirse."

Farewells were hastily exchanged and they headed off. Moses let out a long sigh of relief.

"Oh, it wasn't that bad," Saoirse said. "They seem very nice."

"That's what I'm trying to get my head around."

Five minutes later, they were in Leonardo's cafe. It was quiet, with only three tables occupied. At one, four exhausted-looking, young office guys in expensive suits and cheap haircuts were analysing why they had failed to have any luck with women all evening. Their argument essentially was that they had failed to meet any woman worthy of them. They convinced themselves that their failure was a success.

At another table, a middle-aged couple sat in comfortable, familiar silence. The woman, wearing a purple dress and black jacket, was thoughtfully tapping a cup of coffee, gazing idly at the people passing by on the street. Her husband, in blue jeans and a white Neil Young T-shirt, chewed a hamburger and occasionally fidgeted with his Poirot moustache.

At another table, a young man sat alone, reading an early edition of the newspaper. He wore a black jumper and tan slacks and looked up hopefully every time someone walked past his table.

The light in the cafe was harsh, making the red chairs, white tables and blue-tiled floor glare vividly. Moses and Saoirse went to a table at the back of the room, where the light was less severe. They exchanged small talk after ordering their food. Saoirse sipped orange juice through a straw, glancing around the restaurant. Moses toyed with his glass of Coke. The silence hadn't become uncomfortable yet.

Vivaldi's "Spring" was fluttering in Moses's brain again. He stared into the dark, fizzing bubbles of his Coke and saw himself and Saoirse dancing to the orchestra again. The tables and chairs had disappeared as they glided across the blue floor.

The middle-aged couple were also dancing around the cafe. The young man in the black jumper was dancing with the waitress. The four suited guys eventually paired off with each other and were also dancing, gazing longingly into each other's eyes, finally realising the real reason why they had failed to have any luck with women tonight. Outside, couples swished past, dancing, men and women, women and women, men and men, cats and dogs, sticks and leaves…

Moses realised that Saoirse was staring intently at him. The cafe spun back into focus as Vivaldi faded into the sizzle of the grill.

"What?"

"Moses, how often do you drift away into your own little world?"

"Oh, I spend most of my time in my own little world. I just tend to drift back into this one every now and then. The cloud is my home. "

Saoirse continued to stare at him, an unasked question furrowing her brow.

"What is it, Saoirse?"

"This may seem an awkward question, but I... um... are you... like... seeing anyone?"

"Oh! At the moment? No. I was, a while ago, but... eh... well..."

"Are you still carrying a torch?"

"Christ, no," Moses lied, laughing, looking away. "That particular torch has well and truly been blown out. Big time!"

"Good." Saoirse smiled, looking almost satisfied with his answer. "At least we now know where we stand."

"No, we don't. What about you? Are you seeing anyone?"

"I'm not attached, if that's what you mean, Moses. I've kind of given up on men this last year. Most men are complete dickheads."

"Oh fantastic!"

"That's why I was surprised to meet someone I could talk to in Halogen."

"Ah, it's getting better."

"It's nice to meet someone who doesn't make you want to throw up within five minutes of talking to him."

Moses grinned at her. She smiled back for some seconds and then returned her attention to the orange juice, blushing very slightly. She lightly brushed a few stray strands of hair from her forehead.

In that instant, that very second, Moses knew that the connection had been made. He almost felt it click into place. He felt the real adrenaline rush, the sudden clarity. He could see those snow-covered forests in the shimmering moonlight.

He stared at her, sipping her orange juice through the straw. He wanted to kiss her. He wanted to make love to her. There in the cafe, among the lettuce and tomatoes. Mad, frantic, jungle, tribal love. He wanted to throw his clothes off. He wanted to leap naked over the table, Tarzan howling from a jungle vine, and land in her lap. He wanted to –

"Here's your hamburger, sir."

"What?" Moses looked up, startled. "Oh, thanks."

The waitress grunted at him and put the plate on the table.

"I'll get your pizza now, miss."

"That's great." Saoirse smiled. "Thanks."

They exchanged more small talk while they ate. The quality of the food. The weather outside. The variety of clubs in Dublin. Banjo's inability to walk in a straight line.

"I wonder how Razor and your friend are getting on," Saoirse said, after a while. "They seemed to have… em… hit it off."

She looked at her watch for the first time since she'd met Moses. Natalie used to look at hers incessantly.

"I suppose I need to think about getting a taxi home now."

"What's the hurry?" *Don't leave me already!* "Do you have far to go?"

"Ashfield."

"Ashfield? God almighty, that's the back of beyond. Fuck a taxi. You'd need a spaceship to get out there. It's eight miles north of the edge of the universe."

Moses chewed the remains of his hamburger. He wasn't tasting it. His mind was racing.

Maybe I can prevent an alien abduction.

Saoirse looked outside. There were still a lot of people walking around. Some were visibly shivering against the chill. Saoirse turned back to him.

"Can I borrow your phone?" she asked. "Mine died while we were waiting for you to get your jacket from the cloakroom. I want to see if I can link up with Razor and share a taxi home with her."

Moses gave her his phone.

"Thanks."

She pecked a number and waited.

"Hi, Razor … God, you got back already? … How did it, ahem, go? … Oh really? … And when did he pass out? … Yes, it probably is best to let him sleep it off … Anyway, look, I won't be back for a while … ha ha ha … No, nothing like that … Well, I'll have to get a taxi back, I suppose … You never know … I might … Oh, I don't know… ha ha ha … Maybe a bucket of cold water and a hot poker will wake him up … So would that … ha ha ha … See you … Bye."

Saoirse handed the phone back to Moses.

"Okay," she said. "Let's go."

They made their way to the taxi rank. The small talk seemed to have died when they left Leonardo's. Moses was too afraid of saying the wrong thing so he locked up his tongue for the time being. He noted with some small relief that at least Saoirse still seemed to be in a good mood.

"Can you take me to Ashfield, please?" Saoirse asked the taxi driver when they reached the rank.

"Ashfield?" The taxi driver moaned. "Have you any idea how far away that is?"

"It's a bit of a distance," Saoirse replied, taken aback. "But I thought you might be happy for –"

"I'll be ready for my pension by the time we get out to that discarded arsehole of a dump. And ready for my grave by the time I get back into the city."

"Look, if it's too much –"

"No, get in." The taxi driver seemed to be on the verge of tears. "I may as well try to make some money tonight. Otherwise the wife will be devour me when I get home. If I throw some money at her, I might be able to calm her down for a few minutes and sneak off to the bedroom or the shed."

"It's really cold and I'd like –"

"I know how cold it is. She made me sleep out in the shed last night. But at least that was less frosty than the bloody bedroom. Ever since I stood on her hamster, she hasn't had two nice words to say to me."

"It might be quicker for you to just walk to Ashfield, Saoirse," Moses suggested.

"Get in the taxi, love," the driver pleaded. "I'll tell you all about it on our way there. It'll be good to talk to someone. And a lot cheaper than therapy or murder."

Saoirse turned to Moses before getting into the taxi.

The moment of truth!

"So, this was fun." Saoirse smiled. "Thanks for proving once again that white men can't dance."

"You could write a whole chapter on my dance moves!" Moses tried to keep the ecstatic delirium out of his voice. "We can do some more research some time."

"Yeah, I'd like that." Saoirse slid into the taxi seat. "I'll be in touch."

"Great. I'd love to tell you all about the dance moves I learnt at –"

Moses realised that the taxi was already pulling away and the tears were already streaming down the taxi driver's face as he began sobbing his way through his sorry saga.

His mind whirling to its own tribal rhythms, Moses made his way slowly back home. He needed time to calm down. He needed to be alone for a while to process what had happened over the last two hours. Splendid isolation was the goal now.

"Hey, Moses!"

Moses snapped out of his aimless reverie and saw Sandra and Roger walking towards him. Roger was wearing his casual suit and tie. Sandra looked like she was on her way to an ambassador's reception.

What the hell is going on here?

"Why are you walking the streets on your own so late in the evening?" Sandra asked.

"Maybe he's looking for his career path!" Roger laughed heartily until he realised that Sandra wasn't laughing.

"Why are you two walking the streets together so late in the evening?" Moses replied. "Together."

"We're not together," Roger answered, slightly too quickly.

"We've had an… interesting evening together," Sandra clarified.

"Interesting?" Moses couldn't help laughing. "What did you go to? A presentation about millennial marketing for the new dawn?"

Sandra started laughing for the first time, but Roger just glared at Moses.

"Actually, Moses," Roger snarled, "we were at a fascinating lecture about Mesopotamian pottery at the library. It's amazing what you can learn from a few cracked pots, isn't it, Sandra?"

"Oh yes, you can learn loads from cracked pots. Just think of all we've learnt from that crackpot coconut in the office."

"You really know how to show a girl a good time, Roger!" Moses couldn't help smirking. "Did you spend the rest of the evening watching documentaries about antelopes?"

"I wasn't showing any girl a good time," Roger snapped. He didn't notice the sharp look Sandra gave him. "We just both happened to be free when Sandra asked me if I had any plans for the weekend."

"Oh, so Sandra did the asking." Moses nodded his head slowly, grinning at Sandra. "That clarifies a lot."

"At least we did something useful with our evening," Sandra replied. "I supposed you spent it getting locked with that Banjo down in Halogen again."

"Actually, I had a great…" Moses realised that the last people he wanted to talk to about the evening were Roger and Sandra. They would be able to shatter the magic with just a few toxic words. "Yeah, Banjo and I got locked. But I finally unlocked myself from the farce and decided to make my way home."

"Anyway, we'd love to spend the whole night talking to you," Roger said with a shudder, "but life's too precious. We'll see you on Monday if you remember to come into the office."

"Try to get your hangover sorted out by then," Sandra cautioned as they walked away. "Don't give Coconut any excuses to swing the axe. The office would be boring without you."

Moses was glad to see the pair melt away into the drunken crowd. All he cared about tonight was holding on to the memory of the magical tribal dance with Saoirse. His career could wait until another day. He could only stumble along one path at a time.

I like to stir it up, baby. I'm the whiskey in your lemonade.
I'll call round this evening with the cucumbers and marmalade.
I wanna drop some sugar in your cup of tea,
I wanna taste your honey, little stingin' bee.
Save me from the white man dancin' blues

White Man Dancin' Blues
Fingers Flaherty

Half an hour later, the path finally led to Ellington House. Moses staggered into his apartment and threw his jacket on the floor. He went down to his bedroom and opened the door, ready to collapse on to the sheets.

But Floyd was sitting on Moses's bed, wearing paisley boxer shorts and a white "Elvis Lives" vest. He was intently reading a small magazine called *Playsquirrel*. He jumped up when Moses lurched into the room.

"Jesus Christ, Moses," he said guiltily. "You could have knocked."

"Why would I knock coming into my own bedroom?" Moses sat beside Floyd on the bed and waited for the bedroom to stop spinning. Floyd sat on the magazine. "Listen. I need some advice."

"You seemed to be getting along fine without any help… I was watching you in the nightclub."

"You were in Halogen? I didn't see you there."

"Well, you could barely see the end of your noses, Moses. Anyway, I lost you in the crowd. I had a few bottles at the bar."

"Were you locked out of your tree, ha ha ha?"

"I'm not drunk enough to find that joke funny! Yes, I was in Halogen and I went on to the dance floor. And just when I was finally getting to boogie away to my furry heart's content, some cloven-hoofed, twenty-stone, bog-hopping, sheep-shagging culchie nearly trampled me into the ground. I don't know if he was dancing or trying to wriggle a wasp out of his trousers. Ignorant red-neck bastard landed right on my tail. I decided to hobble to a table to recover and plot my revenge on the inbred wanker. Then who should I see kissing the face off this girl in a red dress –"

"Yes, okay, Floyd." Moses realised he was blushing. "I kinda got lucky."

"It sure looked that way. A nice-looking girl. Though admittedly, she's not my cup of tea."

"She wouldn't be, I suppose. She's too big. And doesn't have a bushy tail."

"Maybe she does have a bushy tail." Floyd laughed. "She's just hiding it. So what happens now, Moses?"

"I've reached a bit of a… situation." Moses took out a cigarette. "I'm at a crossroads… The road is too dark for me to know which way to go… Perhaps I need –"

"Did you go to a seminar on Robert Frost on the way home? Try to get to the point before the morning sun begins to rise majestically in the east."

"Is this the start of a glorious new morning?" Moses lit the cigarette, deep in thought. "Or is it still the same dark night of the soul? Or then again maybe she… It's hard to know… Then again…"

Floyd started laughing. He accidentally swallowed a mouthful of smoke. His laughter segued into a spluttering coughing fit.

"What's so funny?" Moses growled. "I'll stub this cigarette out on your tail if you don't wise up."

"You always have to take time out and have paralysis by analysis. Or, in your case, rigor mortis by analysis."

"All I ask for is a steady, happy relationship, Floyd." Moses moodily stubbed out his cigarette. "Something that will help me get Natalie out of my system. Is that too much to ask for from life? I really think I'm on to something with Saoirse. I think we have the chance of a… something that might –"

"Go fuck yourself, you lousy bastard," a female voice roared from across the hall. "You're nothing but a slimy two-faced prick. You should be locked up. In the fucking zoo!"

"What the hell is that?" asked Floyd.

"That'd be Tiffany," Moses said.

"Listen to me, you stupid, contrary, psychotic bitch. I was just trying to brush the ash off her blouse. I didn't mean to rub."

"And that'd be Bill."

"Where the fuck am I suppose to sleep, Tiffany?"

"I don't care. Why don't you curl up into that whore's blouse? You seem to already know your way around it."

"You're paranoid! That's your problem."

"And you're a degenerate arsehole. That's yours."

Moses stood up and tried to rein in his galloping thoughts. He went into the bathroom and splashed some cold water on his face. He stared at his blurred reflection for some minutes, trying to visualise some sort of future for himself and Saoirse. Nothing would come into focus. Soon the crossroads was spinning in front of him. It was time to go sleep.

He walked back to the bedroom, eager to hear what further advice Floyd might have for him.

Floyd was sprawled on Moses's blanket, fast asleep. *Playsquirrel* lay open beneath him. Moses picked the sleeping squirrel up by the tail. Floyd grunted and kicked in his sleep. He put Floyd down on a cushion on the floor. He threw a handkerchief over him.

As Moses drifted off to sleep, he saw a bright light beginning to shine on the crossroads.

However, the light made the shadows even darker.

Slipping into his dreams, Moses wondered what was lurking in those shadows.

When you gasp for breath on your pillow, it's not my name you're calling.
You cry out in your dreams, but it's not into my arms you're falling.

The day is getting' dark, the moon is getting' brighter.
My feet feel heavy, but my heart is getting' lighter,
Walkin' away from the white man dancin' blues.

White Man Dancin' Blues
Fingers Flaherty

Chapter 8

And Floyd Makes Three

I still don't take the hint, no matter how many times I'm rejected.
I'll never take your hint, baby, no matter how often I'm rejected.
So long as I can think of you, I'll never feel neglected.
She cut off my water, she blew my fuse.
Looks like I'm in for a blacker shade of the blues.

Blacker Shade Of Blue
Fingers Flaherty

"Rejection!"

Coconut Fred paused dramatically and looked around the meeting room.

"That is what I am talking about this morning. Rejection. Why it is our enemy. Know your enemy, folks! Sing his tune. And then you will be able to defeat him."

No one was singing in the meeting room. It was 9.00 on Friday morning and time for the weekly motivation meeting. Moses hadn't had his breakfast. Paul looked like he hadn't had his sleep. Sandra's attention was focused exclusively on the progress of the hands on her watch. Lydia nodded absently, her eyes gazing on the horizon of some distant planet. Roger looked like he was mentally trying to solve a complex quadratic equation while chewing meditatively on a rotten lemon. Every time Roger caught Sandra's eye, he looked the other way.

Fred rubbed his hands together, warming to the sound of his own voice. Unlike the others, he looked to be scrubbed and energised, his eyes sparkling with slightly demented enthusiasm.

"Know your enemy and sing his tune," Fred continued. "Moses, what do you think I mean?"

Moses wished he hadn't spent the last five minutes thinking about something Saoirse had said the previous evening.

"Um… well, Fred, what I… ahem… think is… em…"

"…that you should have been paying closer attention," Fred snapped. "God almighty, I feel like I'm addressing the mute branch of the undertakers' union. Lydia, you get the ball rolling."

Lydia was now staring at her wrist, a small smile dangling from her lips, oblivious to the roomful of stares.

"Lydia!" Fred shouted.

"What?" Lydia jumped slightly. "Me?"

"Oh, for heaven's sake!" Fred glared around the room. "Paul, what do you… No, never mind. They'll be excavating our skeletons by the time we get an answer from you. Sandra, can you get us off the runway?"

"I'm afraid I don't understand your question." Sandra smiled. "Could you perhaps repeat it?"

"Am I speaking in some alien tongue today? As I said, we have to know our enemy and sing his tune. What does that mean?"

The room fell silent again. Everyone examined their knuckles. Lydia was again smiling gently to herself. Roger's head was bobbing to an internal rhythm. Sandra was gazing out the window, a slightly puzzled frown on her face. Paul's face was a study of exhausted boredom.

Fred took a few seconds to mentally marshal his thoughts.

"I may as well do all the talking." He sighed. "Otherwise, we'll be eligible for our pensions before the meeting ends. Our greatest enemy is rejection in the marketplace. Especially during the current economic readjustment. Do you all follow me?"

The room silently nodded its head.

Saoirse's words continued to wriggle inside Moses's head, no matter how much he tried to shake them out.

"Rejection," continued Fred, building up a head of steam, "is the enemy. And to defeat rejection, we must understand it. Sing its tune."

Everyone nodded. Paul's nod looked to be in danger of dislocating his head from his shoulders. Lydia was still smiling at the horizon, idly stroking her left arm.

"…that could be understood as inner rejection. Self-rejection, even. Self-abuse, if you will. The silent rejection that eats away at our morale. We need to optimise the positive work ethic that we leverage in this company. The spark that brings our clay to life. The raspberry ripple that distinguishes us from the vanilla."

The spark in the room was silent.

Outside, the clay in the flower beds was still.

I think I'll meet Jesse for lunch. I'll phone him once this meeting is over. Assuming phones are still in existence then.

"…sparks getting lost in water. We must continue to hug the flames of adventure." The evangelical side of Fred was coming to the fore. "We are never afraid to push the envelope up the flagpole. Lydia, quit smiling to yourself! It's disturbing to look at."

Lydia cast her eyes down with a mortified blush.

"So, who is he?" Sandra asked, turning to her.

"Who?" Lydia muttered.

"The precious angel you were with last night who has obviously turned you into such a dreamy drip this morning. You look like you found Prince Charming hopping behind the butter in your fridge." Sandra glanced over at Roger. "We all find Prince Charming in the most unlikely of places."

"Oh, it's nothing like that." Lydia laughed, glancing out the window. "I'm just... in a good mood this morning. My life isn't that interesting, you know."

"I'm sure it isn't!" Fred had a distant look on his face. "It's a bloody distraction, though. Anyway, as I was saying..."

Moses's mind began to wander relentlessly again. He started thinking about Saoirse. It was three weeks since the tribal dance in Halogen, and he still wasn't sure where things were between the two of them.

"...is very important, of course, but Moses sadly doesn't realise that because he has drifted off to the cloud yet again! Are we keeping you from something more important, Moses?"

Moses stared at Fred, hopelessly lost. His brain refused to even try to look for a sensible answer.

"That's okay, Moses," Fred said. "I don't mind wasting my breath trying to motivate someone who this morning seems to have completely lost all understanding of why he's even here! You'll have plenty of time to cuddle your thoughts when you're in the dole queue! Anyway, we'll call this meeting to a close. Does anyone have any questions?"

The shuffling chairs gave no answer.

Moses ran outside to get some fresh air and clear his head with a smoke.

Floyd was standing outside the building, wearing an orange hoodie and a blindingly white shirt.

"Did you hear all that shite, Floyd?"

"I heard some of it. Then I decided I'd hear more sense by listening to the leaves idly rustling in the trees."

"Haven't you got better things to be doing with your time?"

"I could see through the window that you were all lost and confused. I thought it best to check in with you." Floyd's smile was as dazzling as his shirt. "After all, it's my sacred mission to get you back on track. Nothing in life happens by accident. I didn't just fall out of some tree into your life, you know… Actually, come to think of it, that morning I met you on Cartright Road, I had fallen out of a tree and into that bush, but that's not the point."

"Is there likely to be a point? Or is this going to be another meeting from hell?"

"You were no great shakes yourself that morning, if I remember right. Vomiting all over the pavement like a fire hose. You seem to think that you magically invented me out of thin air."

"Floyd, it's too early in the day for your existential conundrums."

Moses had his own existential conundrums to work out. He wasn't sure if he was still going out with Saoirse. Were the last three weeks with her just a dream? Was she just a dream? Moses hoped a hard drag on the cigarette would blast away the cobwebs in his brain. It didn't.

"Women are strange, Floyd. It's hard to read them –"

"How are things with Saoirse?"

"Oh, that." Moses wasn't sure he wanted to get into this. "Just… the usual."

"The usual? You wouldn't care to be a bit more specific there, would you, Moses?"

"Me and Saoirse had… um… words last night, Floyd."

"I see." The squirrel laughed. "Words can be a bastard. Unfortunately, we're stuck with them. Conversation, for example, is pretty much pointless without them."

"To be more specific, then, we had an argument. It was our first real argument. No, not even an argument. More of a misunderstanding. It was more a case of us having different definitions of –"

"Moses," Floyd sighed, "am I likely to have grandchildren before you get to the point of this story?"

"It can be very hard to understand people." Moses gazed at the smoke dispersing in front of his face. "Everyone puts their own spin on everything."

"Your problem is that you're always trying to build some golden calf," said Floyd, walking away, "while you're rejecting the real deal that is chewing the cud right in front of you."

"Saoirse doesn't chew the cud!"

Moses stamped out the cigarette with a frown. Nothing would surprise him about Saoirse anymore.

She's a sidewalk angel, but you should see her behind the curtain,
She's an angel on the sidewalk, but wait until you get her behind that curtain.

Spend half an hour in her bed and you'll soon know why I'm hurtin'.
I've lost even more than I thought I could lose,
Sittin' here with nothin' but a blacker shade of the blues.

Blacker Shade Of Blue
Fingers Flaherty

Kilroy Park was crowded, the sun splashing down gently on office workers.

Moses and Jesse were sitting on the grass, staring up into the sky, chewing meditatively on their lunch. Moses was already beginning to feel better. The sun felt warm on his face, a gentle breeze taking the sting out of it. His beetroot and egg sandwich was digesting comfortably.

Some people had already begun to leave the park, jackets slung carefree across their shoulders. Others showed absolutely no inclination to start moving.

Moses recognised a few people. A group from the Accounts department seemed to be having a picnic of sorts, complete with food, drinks and *The Financial Times*. Close by, Lydia was having what looked like an intimate talk with some guy who worked in Aztech's Programming division. She was gently putting crisps into the programmer's mouth and laughing. Near the edge of the park, Aztech's sales manager was sitting alone in his car, listening to the radio. Hash smoke and The Beatles' "Sexy Sadie" drifted through his open window.

"You know, Jesse, I sometimes wonder –"

"How's Saoirse, Moses?" Jesse interrupted.

"If you must know, we had a bit of a disagreement," Moses

admitted. "Yesterday evening."

"Over what?"

"Oh, over this and that." Moses shrugged, watching the crisp-eating couple. "And the other."

"Yes, it's always the specifics that bust up relationships." Jesse nodded. "People can live with vagueness for years. Except Bubbles, of course. That girl doesn't allow much vagueness in her life. I feel sorry for her next conquest! She was on the phone to Lucy for an hour last night. Why does everyone think that their own little problems are fascinating to everyone else?"

Lydia threw a crisp in the air. The programmer opened his mouth to catch it, but the crisp hit his forehead and bounced on the grass. They both laughed loudly, falling into each other. Sure of themselves. Certain of where they were in their relationship.

Some of the accountants raised their eyes from *The Financial Times* to see what the commotion was.

The car radio was now playing "Lola" as the smoke dispersed.

The programmer checked his watch and stood up. He bent back down to kiss Lydia. He put on his jacket and started walking back to the office, Lydia looking after him for some seconds. She checked her watch and shrugged to herself. She fumbled in her jacket and took out a cigarette. She sat there smoking, staring gently into the grass, a relaxed smile curling on her lips.

"Saoirse's problem at the moment," Moses said, reaching for his own packet of cigarettes, "is that I'm not committed enough."

"It's a bit early to talk about commitment, isn't it?" Jesse remarked.

"We were both a bit stoned at the time. She said something about not wanting to go out with some haunted ghost. She wanted something more substantial."

The sales manager was now walking across the park. He had an unlit cigarette in his hands. Moses recoiled slightly as the dark suit walked past him, stung by the sharp smell of his cheap aftershave.

"God knows what she meant." Moses shrugged. "It's hard to find the answer when you don't know what the question is."

The sales manager walked over to Lydia. She glanced up when his shadow fell across her face. She winced slightly as he drew closer, her nose crinkling. He held up his unlit cigarette.

"The path to true love never runs straight, Moses," Jesse declared solemnly.

"Is that your advice?" Moses tapped his ash into the grass. "That was well worth waiting for!"

Meanwhile, the sales manager was smoking his cigarette, slowly, talking to Lydia. She looked around the park, uneasily. Then she got up from the grass, putting on her jacket, smiling politely, glancing around anxiously.

"He thinks he's in with a chance with her because she's on her own," Moses said, pointing to the salesman. "He's waiting for her to fall at his feet in gratitude."

Lydia walked away, quickly. The sales manager followed her for some seconds and then gave up the chase.

"Why don't you and Saoirse come round to my place this weekend?" Jesse suggested. "It would be nice to get to know her properly."

"Sounds like a good idea," Moses agreed. "I'll just check with

Saoirse to see if she wants to do it."

"Why on earth wouldn't she want to do it?"

"I don't always understand her. It sometimes feels like she's always wearing fancy dress." Moses glanced down at his watch. "Oh Christ, I'm late back for the office. God only knows what horrors Fred has in store for me."

I saw them this morning, the prince and the king.
Having breakfast in my kitchen, woman, were the prince and the king.
And then you have the nerve to ask why I can't understand anything.
I'll drive a pauper's limousine by the time I've paid my dues.
I'm all shook up with a blacker shade of the blues.

Blacker Shade Of Blue
Fingers Flaherty

Later that afternoon, Moses was getting coffee in the canteen when his mobile phone rang in his pocket.

"Hello?" *Can't even get a bloody cup of coffee without someone looking for me!* "Moses MacNamara speaking."

"Moses, it's Tiffany."

"Oh, hi…" *What on earth does she want with me?* "How are things?"

"As good as can be expected when you're working with a gaggle of headless monkeys. Anyway, listen, I need a quick favour."

Moses glanced around the canteen. He noticed Lydia sitting at a table with her programmer boyfriend. He wondered if she'd told him about the sales manager. She looked ill at ease.

"Sure." *As long as it doesn't involve me dressing up as a woman.* "What is it?"

The programmer seemed to be asking Lydia a relentless series of questions. He looked concerned. Then suspicious. She shrugged back at him with obvious impatience, staring into her coffee, twirling her cigarette lighter in her hands.

"Do you know any good fancy dress shops in town?" Tiffany asked. "I remember you talking one time about a fancy dress party you went to at college. You all got dressed up as Shakespeare characters and got pissed and went on a bit of a rampage in Finlay Square. That story always stuck with me."

"I was Hamlet." Moses smiled, vividly remembering that night. "We all started playing football with the plastic skull. Lucky we weren't all arrested. Anyway, why are you looking for a fancy dress shop?"

"Bill and I tried some role-playing a while back and it ended up being a bit of a… disaster. However, we've agreed to give it another go. You can't give up on things just because they go wrong sometimes, can you? Otherwise you'd give up on everything eventually."

"I suppose." *I've given up on everything long ago.* "So what's the plan this time?"

"Well, Bill seemed to like my nurse's outfit last time. However, I'd like to get a really special one this time. One that might spark his engine a bit."

The programmer finished his bottle of water and stood up. He asked Lydia one last question. She looked up at him and shrugged. He stared down at her for some seconds, then stormed off. She looked at her lighter, gently shaking her head in confusion. She finished her cup of coffee and went after him.

"It might be dangerous to have too many sparks around Bill." Moses laughed. "He always seems to be on the brink of combusting. Anyway, the best place is Wrap Around on Sugar Street."

"Thanks, Moses. You know, I think this experiment will be interesting. It'll be fun to see Bill's mouton dressed up as lamb, so to speak."

"Goodbye then, Tiffany."

Moses lifted his cup of coffee and headed back to his desk, hoping he might find some sanity there.

You can dress me up, woman. I wanna be your mannequin.
Change my clothes, woman, and play with your mannequin.
But when you take out them handcuffs, that's when I start panickin'.
You won't be satisfied until we're on the news
Tellin' the world about our blacker shade of the blues.

Blacker Shade Of Blue
Fingers Flaherty

At 4.00, Moses found the courage to phone Saoirse.

Her phone rang for some seconds.

"Hello?" Saoirse said.

"Saoirse, it's Moses. How are you?"

"Fine. Yeah. I think so. I suppose. Probably. Well, no, not really."

"Oh?" *She'll be talking backwards next!* "What's wrong?"

"I'm not long out of bed."

"It's 4.00 in the afternoon! Did someone tie you to the bed?"

"I've just been a bit exhausted lately, Moses."

"I suppose," Moses agreed. "The weather has been very clammy lately —"

"It's got nothing to do with the weather."

Moses stared at his computer screen, looking for inspiration. He hoped Paul wasn't eavesdropping on this conversation. He glanced over, but Paul was totally engrossed in the data sweeping across his smartphone.

Moses tried to read what was on Paul's screen, to see what warranted such mental exertion. It turned out to be Angry Birds.

"Moses," Saoirse prompted. "Are we going to get this conversation up and running?"

"How has the thesis been coming along today, now that you've dragged yourself out of bed?" Moses asked. "Are any white men dancing today?"

"Guess so," she said, indifferently. "I hope to get a new chapter started today."

"I think even Paul could muster up more enthusiasm than that."

"Don't mind me." She yawned. "I'm just… em… whatever…"

Shit. Trouble stirring on the horizon. Time to tackle the issue. No aimless tangents.

"So," Moses asked, "what's the new chapter about?"

"This and that." She sounded even less eager than before. "I'll be exploring hero myths in imperial and nationalist discourse. Looking at how they… things don't quite work… you put people on pedestals… and… um…"

Silence dangled uneasily.

"You sound… withdrawn, Saoirse." *And slightly insane.* "What's up?"

"Well, I've been stressed out about a lot of things the last few days. It's just... I've been wondering..."

"Stressed?" Moses yelped. "This is the first I've heard about people being stressed. No one mentioned about stress to me. Where did all this –"

"Moses, shut up! I was just saying that I've been stressed the last few days. It's not you... Well, it's not just you. It's the thesis. It's other stuff."

"I understand," Moses lied. This conversation was turning into water. "Well, whatever I can do..."

Paul had drifted into a peaceful slumber at the next desk, contented drool dripping down on his smartphone screen.

"We might need to slow things down for a bit," Saoirse was saying, sounding as if she was hesitantly tasting each word before speaking it. "Work out exactly where we are."

"I'm not sure I understand you." Moses laughed, weakly. "Don't take it personally. I don't understand most things."

"Just try to work out where you want to go. You can't sit on the fence forever, Moses. It might be an electric fence."

"I see." Moses didn't even try to sound certain. "That's nice and clear."

"I'll see you tomorrow evening." Saoirse sounded relieved to have found an exit route from the conversation. "Take care of yourself."

"Fine." Moses switched off his phone. "Whatever."

At least this day can't get any more complicated.

An e-mail arrived from Fred, asking Moses to meet him in an hour.

I don't speak your language, baby, I can't see inside your brain.
If I can't speak your language, then I can't see inside your brain.
You're just babbling', baby, like a monkey on cocaine.
I thought she'd kneel down and polish my shoes,
But she just kicked me into a blacker shade of the blues.

Blacker Shade Of Blue
Fingers Flaherty

"You don't know what had Lydia so tickly this morning, do you, Moses?" Fred asked.

"Um… no, Fred," Moses answered, slightly thrown. "I didn't notice –"

"There was obviously something stirring her water. She never acts like that unless she has… has… someone special. It's a bit of a pain to have to deal with."

"I understand." *The bastard's jealous! He's carrying a torch for her and he's jealous that someone else is tickling her feathers. He must have got the sales manager to spy on her. Whatever next?* "Like I said, I was too busy –"

"Now you're just being ridiculous!" Fred opened a drawer in his desk and began impatiently rummaging in it. "You don't even know how to be busy."

Moses gazed out the window. The day was beginning to show the first grey shadows of winding down. A few cars had already left the car park. A slight chill drifted in through Fred's open window.

"Did you leave your tongue at your cubicle, Moses?" Fred asked, head bent into the drawer.

Well, what the fuck do you want me to say? Repeat the Gettysburg Address?

"I… em… wasn't aware that you were waiting for an answer, Fred."

"I wasn't waiting with bated breath. But you could say something to pass the time while I search for… what I'm looking for."

Moses noticed that Fred seemed to be unusually dishevelled. His purple shirt was open at the neck, his tie hanging at an awkward angle. His jacket was flung carelessly over his chair. Even his normally immaculately parted hair showed signs of unaware disturbance.

"It's getting a bit cold these evenings," Moses declared, after searching in vain for an interesting topic of conversation. "Touch of winter beginning to creep –"

"Jesus, Moses, I'd hate to be stuck in a lift with you! Have you heard no whisperings about what's going on with Lydia? I'm just concerned that it might… negatively impact her performance."

Yeah, right! And I'm Abraham Lincoln in a green polka-dot shirt.

Moses's eyes widened when he saw Fred place a bottle of vodka on his desk.

Fred opened the bottle, staring at Moses, apparently daring him to comment. He opened another drawer and dug out two plastic cups and placed them on the desk.

"So, Moses, will you join me in a drink at the end of the day?"

"Um… er… No, thanks… I don't usually –"

"Sit down!" Fred barked. "Don't be a limp dick all your life! Have a glass with me and listen closely to me because I have some good news for you."

Moses sat down. He noticed two more cars leaving the car park.

"Perhaps we shouldn't care," Fred declared, pouring two cups of neat vodka. "Who knows? Perhaps we're better off not knowing."

"Perhaps…" Moses nodded. "True… I'm sorry, Fred. I don't quite follow you."

"Lydia. We're probably better off not knowing what has got into her. And who put it in… It's a personal issue, not a staff issue, at the end of the day. Correct?"

"Oh, right." *Sweet Jesus, is he going to keep me here all night to discuss this? I'd better not tell him about the crisp-eating programmer.* "Yes, maybe it's none of our business."

"Exactly!" Fred took a deep swallow of vodka and shivered. "That vodka is not going to drink itself."

Moses sipped his drink, wincing slightly as the taste flooded his mouth and stung his stomach. He noticed that Fred's cup was nearly empty already.

Another car left the car park.

Fred looked lost in dark thought, scowling into his vodka.

With a silent effort, Moses drank more vodka.

Fred's carrying a torch for Lydia. Sandra's carrying a torch for Roger. Roger's carrying a torch for himself. And Paul's too lazy to carry any torches at all. Who the hell am I carrying a torch for?

"Anyway," Fred said, visibly shaking himself out of his reverie, "I just wanted to tell you that… How can I put this? I have… noticed recently a slight… slight, mind you… a very slight upward curve in your performance graph."

"Really?" Moses steadied himself on his chair, expecting the centre of the universe to evaporate. "I see. Thank you."

"Now, don't start riding your high horse yet." Fred poured himself another cup of vodka. "I want to make my meaning absolutely clear here. Even clearer than usual! You're doing an acceptable job, relatively speaking. The tangible aspects of your performance were never really at issue —"

"Thank you for —"

"Don't interrupt me! I don't want to have to go through this more than once. It's the intangible aspects of your job that I want to concentrate on."

Moses took another sip of vodka.

"Your attitude over the last number of weeks has… improved. Some people might point out that the improvement could be said to be almost imperceptible and some people might be right some of the time… But a vague improvement of sorts on some level is definitely not nonexistent."

"It's good to get positive feedback." *Thank you very much, you cantankerous, begrudging fucker. This must be eating you up.* "I have been trying to… um… get it together, I suppose."

"Don't go dancing in the streets about it. It's hardly going to impact the share price or reverse this fucking recession. However, my superiors, in their infinite wisdom, constantly whinge that we have to encourage all improvement in our human capital resources. No matter how extremely slight that tiny improvement is."

"Well, it's good to know that I'm on the right path."

The only car remaining in the car park was Fred's green Ford Escort. A security guard began making his rounds.

"It's sometimes hard to know the right path." Fred took a swallow of vodka. "That's what my talk this morning was about."

"Really?"

"Wasn't it obvious?"

"There were… eh… a number of possible interpretations of it," Moses stammered. "I think each of us took our own message from it."

"Our path is clear. We must face the enemy. We must know who… what we're up against. Take your eye off the ball and you might find yourself standing alone in the last piss-house on earth with your dick in your hand, not knowing what to do with it."

Moses squirmed slightly at the memory.

"That, Moses, is the challenge! Do you even begin to grasp what I am talking about?"

"Yes." Moses decided it was time for more vodka. "We can't sit on the fence, because it might be an electric fence."

Fred sighed and rubbed his eyes. He suddenly looked very tired. And drunk.

"That's one way of putting it. Once you know which path you're supposed to be following, your balls won't get fried. Can I ask you something?"

No! I want to go home and get the hell away from you because you are beginning to give me the fucking creeps.

"Yes, Fred."

Fred put the lid back on the vodka bottle and put the bottle back in the drawer. He finished the remainder of his cup in one gulp and threw the cup towards his bin.

"I was just wondering," he said, the edges of his words beginning to slur slightly, "if there was any particular reason for your improved performance."

"I don't quite follow you."

"It's perfectly simple! Up to about a month ago, you had a piss-poor attitude to your job. You still do, but at least you don't make it so obvious any more. What has happened to help you turn the corner? I'd like to think that it was because of my motivational, inspirational management, but I'm not that fucking naive. I don't know how much of what I say makes it through to your wavelength."

"I suppose I'm… just a happier person," Moses mumbled. "I had a few problems in my personal life recently, but they seem to be easing out now. To an extent."

"We all have our shit to deal with, so don't go thinking you're special in that regard." Fred rubbed his flushed face. "To be honest, once it doesn't impact operational performance, I couldn't give a flying Eskimo fuck what problems people are going home to."

"Anyway," said Moses, standing up, "I really must be going. I have stuff I want to finish before I head off home. And it's getting late."

"We might be able to build something worthwhile out of you yet. More than can be said for that Paul wreckage beside you. I swear to Jesus, I'm going to ram a white-hot cattle prod up his hole one of these days… Are you sure you don't know what's going on with Lydia? I'd hate to see her personal problems affecting her performance."

"No," Moses replied. "Is it okay if I go now?"

"Sure," Fred muttered, with a dismissive wave. "I'll see you on Monday. Don't be late. Or hungover. Yet again."

Moses turned and walked quickly back to his cubicle. Behind him, he could hear Fred re-opening the drawer and taking out the vodka bottle.

The light was still on in Fred's office when Moses left the building twenty minutes later.

The flame I carried for you, it set my trousers alight.
That damn flame I had for you, it went and set my trousers alight.
At least you'll be able to see me in the dead of the night.
I crawled to your room, but I couldn't pass the queues,
They were lining up with a blacker shade of the blues.

Blacker Shade Of Blue
Fingers Flaherty

Moses was walking out the door on Saturday evening when his phone started ringing.

"Hello?" he said, picking up the phone.

"Hello, Moses. It's Dad."

"Oh, hello." *Blast!* "How… are things?"

"Really fine." Bernard MacNamara sounded unusually casual, chirpy almost, Floyd-like even. "After a busy week, we can all relax. Isn't that so?"

"I… suppose." Moses glanced at his watch. "Was there anything in particular?"

"Actually, I was wondering if you wanted to meet up for lunch tomorrow."

"Do you mind," Moses suggested, cautiously, "if we… perhaps… maybe give it… you know… give it a miss?"

"Okay, Moses," Bernard chirped. "That's no problem."

"What?" *There's something not right here. He should be at least screaming at me by now. If not actually breathing fire down the line.* "Are you sure?"

"Yes. To be honest next week would probably suit me better, come to think of it… So, how are things with you?" Bernard asked, amiably. "Work treating you good?"

"Yeah." Moses wondered how far he should go with this usually controversial subject. "Quite good at the moment. My boss even praised me yesterday, which was somewhat astonishing, given our… history and all."

"Really?" Bernard sounded delighted by the news. "Maybe you're taking that situation to the next level. And how is the new woman, son?"

"Fine." *This I am not getting into!* "I'm actually meeting her in a few minutes. And Jesse has invited us over for a meal tomorrow… Listen, Dad, can I ask you something?"

"Of course, son."

Moses stared at his watch, wondering how to actually ask what was puzzling him.

"It's just that you seem to be… not that I'm being smart or anything… to be in a very good mood. You sound like you found twenty golden eggs in the frying pan."

"Am I not allowed to be in a good mood?" Bernard laughed. "You make me sound like Genghis Khan with a toothache."

"I just… um… wondered if there was any… special reason why you're so upbeat."

"I've just had a good few days and made a good bit of money and made some new contacts and… It's just been a good week."

New contacts?

"I see." Moses realised that he was getting too comfortable in the conversation. "Anyway, sorry about not being able to meet this weekend. I already sort of made plans for tomorrow that I can't –"

"Don't be fretting over it, Moses." Another burst of laughter from Bernard. "It's not as if I'm going to pine away into nothing without you. I can make other plans, meet other people and have a good weekend too."

Other people?

"Well, if you're sure –"

"Of course. We can touch base next weekend and you can properly bring me up to speed on your news and I can… I can let you know what has been happening here. Anyway, bye now."

"Bye, Dad." *Is he actually relieved that he isn't meeting me?* "I'll call you some day soon."

Moses slowly placed the phone in his pocket, trying to figure out what golden egg had fallen into his father's lap.

She ran away from me, all the way to Sydney,
When she left this house, she ran all the way to Sydney.
She gave me her heart, when I needed a kidney.
Same shit happened to Papa in '36, I guess my troubles are yesterday's news.
She went and left me with a blacker shade of the blues.

Blacker Shade oOf Blue
Fingers Flaherty

The late evening sun shone on Moses and Saoirse as they walked to the Skulldiggery. A cold breeze chilled its way through the leaves and some rain clouds shuffled moodily in the sky.

Saoirse was wearing white jeans and a black Acid Academy T-shirt. She smoked her cigarette in silence, gazing into outer space.

Moses looked at her, trying to decipher what was turning behind her eyes. Her face was a mask, the cigarette dangling silently from her lips, the breeze timidly shivering through her black hair.

Fuck this! I might as well be trying to decipher Egyptian hieroglyphics in the dark while hanging upside-down…

"So tell me, what has been going on in the thesis these days? When I was talking to you yesterday, it had been giving you trouble."

"Yeah." Saoirse threw away her cigarette. Her eyes twitched as some of the smoke blew back in her face. "It comes and goes. I'm exploring the different myths that come into play when imperialism and nationalism spark off each other. Myths of the conqueror. Myths of the conquered. Each myth getting rewritten to a particular agenda. Just look at how Jesus keeps changing though history. Jesus the soldier during World War One. Jesus the socialist in the Red '30s. Jesus the hippie in the '60s. Jesus the psychoanalyst in the '80s. Jesus the politically correct new man in the '90s."

"Don't forget Jesus the Vegas Superstar." Moses laughed. "Did you know that Elvis, Hitler and Jesus were the three greatest showmen in history? A formidable trinity!"

"And that's just one example." Saoirse nodded, smiling. "Every myth gets rewritten to serve the needs of someone. Which, I suppose, happens on an everyday level as well."

Shit! Time to go dancing through the minefield.

"In what way?" Moses gazed into the leaves of a nearby tree. "I didn't realise that we were a myth already."

"Moses, you're staring into the tree as if you're going to find the meaning of life scratched into the bark. Are you having an Isaac Newton moment?" The levity in Saoirse's voice sounded forced. "Perhaps I should have brought some apples."

"I'm just staring at… nothing." *Well, that really helped to clarify the situation!* "I'm just… um… thinking."

"You see, that's the problem."

"The tree?" Moses did not feel ready to grasp the nettle. The small talk was now precious. "Leaf it out of this."

Saoirse sighed and reached for another cigarette. She nearly tore it as she snatched it from the packet. She dragged heavily on the smoke when she finally got the cigarette lit.

Moses counted the leaves.

"Okay, Saoirse. I'll try to be serious for the next thirty seconds. What is the problem?"

"I don't know." A small cloud of smoke lingered at her lips. "I honestly don't."

"How much blow did you smoke before coming out here tonight,? It must have been enough to raise the price on the streets. You are making absolutely no sense!"

"It's as simple as this, Moses." She searched his face, peering into his eyes. "I never know exactly what you are looking for. I don't know what you want. I don't think you even know. I'm not trying to solve the riddle of existence. I just want to find out what you want. I sometimes feel like you're just with me while you're waiting for someone else to come along… or come back."

"It'd probably be easier to solve the riddle of existence." Moses tried to laugh, but it strangled in his throat. "Surely you know that by now."

"You don't always have to be a joke... I mean, make a joke." The briefest hint of a smile scurried across Saoirse's lips as she stamped out her cigarette. "Anyway, let's try to have a good evening in the Skulldiggery. No ghosts haunting us."

Moses stopped and kissed her. He realised how terrified he was that he would never hold her this close again. He wanted to tell her that. He wanted to tell her everything he'd thought since he'd met her. Maybe she could help him understand.

Instead, he silently followed her into the nightclub to the table where Banjo was drinking alone.

"You've turned up at last," Banjo declared, delicately pouring his cider from one glass to another. "I thought I was going to have to build some virtual friends to keep me company. Actually, I've spent the last hour on my social media sites. It's the new river of life, the electronic ooze from which a new life form will emerge."

"And are you that new life form?" Saoirse laughed. "The origin of the species?"

"He certainly is one of a kind," Moses said, watching Banjo's shaking hand trying to get the two glasses into contact. "Banjo, take your brain out of its jar and dust it off. You might need it this evening. If you connect it up correctly, you might even alter the course of evolution."

"Evolution's a load of bollocks!" Banjo finally managed to pour his cider into the glass. "We're moving in circles, if not actually moving backwards. The cavemen were probably more intelligent than we are. Rita actually said the cavemen were more intelligent than me!"

"Still plenty of cavemen knocking about," Saoirse said, looking around at the crowd in the Skulldiggery. "Some of these guys should be carrying clubs. That's the only way they'll score."

The Skulldiggery was crammed with the usual Saturday crowd: college graduates and pre-mortgaged office workers. Mobile phones chirped incessantly as text messages zoomed invisibly through the air.

Moses and Saoirse followed Banjo to the upstairs area of the club, looking down on the dance floor. A haze enveloped the dancers. The DJ was playing Fat Boy Slim's "Weapon Of Choice". Some people gyrated on the dance floor, lost to the music. Some people were already slouched against the bar, lost to the world.

"Do you honestly think you'd be happy living all your life on the Internet?" Moses asked Banjo. "Surely you'd shrivel up and die after a few days."

"This is the next stage in evolution," Banjo said. "We are coming down from the trees, people."

"I hate to destroy your illusions, Banjo," Moses laughed, "but most of us came down from the trees a long time ago. Didn't you realise that you were alone up there in the branches?"

"Why on earth would anyone want to live online?" Saoirse asked, gazing down at the dancers. "There's enough in the real world, without having to dabble in the virtual word. Reality's much more interesting than fantasy. You can't cuddle a ghost."

Moses stared at Saoirse, wondering if she was trying to tell him something. She continued to look at the dancers, her head gently nodding.

"Anyway, all that virtual reality stuff is a load of shite," Moses said, glancing at Saoirse. "It can't take the place of real relationships. Real people are much more… complex."

"Have you had any luck while you were waiting for us, Banjo?" Saoirse asked. "Or have you given up on women since Razor threw the bucket of iced water over you that night?"

"I thought I'd had enough of women for now, but then I saw all the talent in here and got my hunting tools out again. However, happiness seems to be hiding in the bushes tonight."

"Happiness is like a meal," Saoirse replied. "No meal is so satisfying that you never go hungry again. No happiness is so complete and perfect that you never get restless again."

"Yeah, but I'm sure that a light snack will tide me over until the morning."

"Anyone want anything from the bar?" Moses looked at Banjo. "Or would you perhaps prefer to download your drinks from the Internet?"

"I don't think so." Banjo glanced at his cider. "I've hardly made a dent in this yet."

"I've seen paralysed budgies drink quicker than you! I'll get you another pint anyway. That'll probably last you the rest of the night."

Saoirse asked for a glass of white wine. Moses stood up and started making his way towards the bar as All Saints' "Pure Shores" started playing.

Moses looked over at the dance floor as he squeezed his way through the crowd. There was barely room to breathe, let alone dance.

Some people looked distinctly uncomfortable in the tight squeeze. Other people looked distinctly delighted.

At the bar, things weren't much better, as people pushed forward, trying to get served. Moses nearly lost his footing in the crush and winced as some woman in a long red dress began roaring her order above the din.

Trying to steady himself, Moses reached forward to grab on to the bar counter.

"A fucking gin and tonic," Red Dress roared at the barman, "and two fucking vodkas, you lousy little retard! I know you can fucking hear me."

Moses turned around to take a closer look at her. She was tall and slim, able to negotiate her way through the elbows and fists and shoulders. Her eyes had the bloodshot blur of an evening's worth of gin and tonics. In the heat of the crowd, her short brown hair seemed to be soaking into her sweating face.

"Over here, you little prick! You got a good eyeful of me earlier, wanker." She suddenly turned her glare on Moses. "And what the fuck are *you* gawping at?"

"Nothing," Moses yelped, recoiling from the ferocity of her stare. He tightened his grip on the counter. "I… um… thought you were someone else."

"I am. Now fuck off!"

Moses closed his eyes, heaving a deep sigh. He vowed not to return to the bar for the rest of the evening.

When Moses opened his eyes again, he realised that it wasn't the bar counter he had been gripping the past few seconds.

His outstretched hand hadn't actually made it as far as the bar. It had come to rest on the shoulder of a stocky, middle-aged skinhead. The skinhead wore a sweaty green T-shirt and black jeans. Moses had been gripping his shoulder all during the trauma with Red Dress.

Just as soon as Moses realised his mistake, the skinhead turned around to face him. Moses hastily withdrew his hand and wondered if he could spontaneously evaporate.

This fascist bastard is going to kill me.

The skinhead did not look angry. In fact, he smiled at Moses, a bottle of beer in one hand, a whisky in the other. He stared into Moses's eyes.

Aw shit!

The skinhead advanced on Moses, still smiling, expectant, his eyes burning.

Moses tried to avoid eye contact, his eyes frantically darting everywhere until he felt dizzy.

The skinhead slowly, very slowly, squeezed past Moses.

For a second, their eyes met. The skinhead smiled again at Moses, his gaze lingering for some seconds.

This evening cannot get any worse!

Trying to break eye contact with the smitten skinhead, Moses cast his eyes back to the bar.

It was then he saw Tony Lyons.

Tony was wearing a white shirt, open halfway down his hairy chest, and talking eagerly to a buxom woman in a tight yellow top. His eyes darted from one breast to the other, as his fingers crawled slowly along the bar, advancing on her.

Is Natalie here?

Moses turned his attention back to the bar and finally signalled to the barman. Grabbing his drinks, he turned to retreat.

He glanced over at Tony again. The buxom woman was leaning into Tony, playing with the buttons on his shirt, laughing up at him. His hand was resting on her shoulder. Massaging it.

Walking back to his seat, Moses scanned the surging crowd, looking for Natalie. The only person he recognised was the skinhead, who smiled back at him, hope flickering in his eyes.

I am never setting foot in this fucking place again!

"You took your time," Banjo grumbled when Moses finally made it back to the table. "Did you get lost on the stairs?"

"It's like Afghanistan at the bar," Moses said, setting the drinks on the table. "Someone tore off my arm in the crush, but I managed to staple it back on."

"What was up with the skinhead?" Saoirse asked. "Did you know him?"

"Who?" *Fucking typical! She would have to see that encounter, wouldn't she?* "The dickhead who nearly knocked me over?"

"Well, he did seem to be standing very close to you."

"Yes, he thought I was someone else." *His shoulder-mate, perhaps.* "But we soon had it sorted out."

"What was up with the wagon in the red dress?" Banjo asked, after a long gulp of his cider. "She gave you a look that would make a volcano think twice about erupting."

"Jesus, you both must have been watching me very closely." *Shit! Did they see me looking around for Natalie?* "I would have done a little dance if I'd known you were both going to be paying such close attention."

"You could have danced with your skinhead friend!" Saoirse laughed. "He seemed to be quite taken with you."

"God almighty, you can bet that if I had to be having a heart attack down there, no one would have been paying a blind bit of attention to me!"

They drank in silence for some minutes, each getting lost in their own thoughts. Banjo was staring intently into his cider. Saoirse was looking at the dancers, a slight smile playing on her lips, her fingers tapping her wine glass in time to REM's "Accelerate".

Moses resumed his search for Natalie. He saw that Tony was now whispering in the woman's ear. She had her hands on his waist, nodding, smiling. That was enough to convince Moses that Natalie was nowhere in the building. However, every time he saw a girl with red hair in the crowd, his heart skipped.

He realised that Saoirse had just asked him a question.

"What?"

"I said that you'd better be careful your eyes don't shoot out of their sockets." Saoirse sounded tetchy. "They're darting around the place like deranged mosquitoes. Who are you looking for?"

"Oh, no one." *Is my face burning up yet?* "I'm just… gazing at the crowd. Anyway, on to more important matters. What shit was Banjo drivelling about while I was at the bar?"

"I was telling Banjo about my thesis." Saoirse took a sip of her wine. "I was explaining to Banjo that history is really just a story that was written by someone. Just like *Alice In Wonderland*. History is nothing more than a series of facts and assumptions and myths. No more real than Wonderland… That's the thing about myths. They help us understand the past."

"Yeah," Moses agreed automatically. He realised that Saoirse was staring at him. "What?"

"Myths help us understand ourselves." There was an edge to her voice. "They explain where we came from… But ultimately, myths are bullshit."

"Of course." *What the hell have we strayed into now?* "I suppose so… Oh, by the way, Jesse's invited us around for a meal tomorrow evening."

"Has he?" There was faint tinge of challenge in Saoirse's voice. "Tomorrow evening?"

Ricky Martin began celebrating la vida loca on the dance floor.

Moses realised that he was on a knife edge. In his attempt to steer the conversation away from the jungle, he had now driven straight into a minefield.

Fuck! If she says that she is not going to Jesse's meal, that's it. There will be no "us" tomorrow evening. I should have let Banjo do all the talking.

Saoirse took another sip of her wine.

Ricky Martin was waking up in New York City, grumbling about his funky hotel.

"What time does he want us to be there?" Saoirse's tone was absolutely non-committal.

"7.00," Moses replied, heart thumping. He reached for his cigarettes but realised that his hand was trembling. He hid his hands under the table. "Will you be able to make it?"

Ricky Martin was complaining that there was a bullet lodged in his brain. His girl had skin the colour of mocha.

The dance floor was a frenzy of movement.

"I should be there at 6.30." A tiny smile flickered across Saoirse's lips. "Maybe later."

"Okay." Moses nodded. He thought his heart would explode with joy.

"Can I come?" Banjo asked.

"What?" Moses had forgotten Banjo was there. "Where?"

"To the dinner?"

"No!"

"Why not?"

"Because you haven't mastered the art of eating with a knife and fork."

Moses looked at the dance floor. He saw a tight, yellow top moving through the crowd. Tony was kissing the woman as they danced. One of her hands disappeared inside his shirt. Around them, the crowd surged.

In a far corner, Moses noticed a woman with red hair. He squinted his eyes against the smoke, trying to make out her face.

Is that Natalie?

The red-haired woman turned around. She was younger than Natalie. Much younger. And her skin was darker. Almost the colour of mocha.

"All myths," Saoirse said, finishing her drink. "And bullshit!"

"What?" Moses turned his gaze away from the dance floor. "Which myths?"

"We invent these stories to understand our past. Because if we don't understand the past, it will never let us go."

"Sure." *Back into the jungle!* "Of course. All parts of Wonderland. Banjo's our guide to Wonderland, these days. Aren't you, Banjo?"

No answer.

Moses turned around. Banjo had fallen asleep, his head sloped back, his mouth wide open.

"I hope the red queen doesn't see you like that." Moses laughed. "One swipe of the axe and she'd have that head clean off you."

"Yes," Saoirse said. "You just never know where these wild women will pop out of."

Moses nervously glanced around the club. The skinhead made eye contact with him and looked disappointed when Moses didn't respond. Tony and his new friend were squeezing through the crowd, making their way off the dance floor, her hand in his back pocket. The woman in the red dress was roaring another order at the young barman.

U2's "Mysterious Ways" began blaring.

This fucking place would do your head in!

Saoirse was nodding her head in time to the song.

"Do you want to dance?" Moses asked her. "This white man feels like venturing into the jungle again."

Saoirse smiled and stood up. They walked down to the dance floor.

She took his hand and led him through the crowd.

On the way, Moses noticed at least six women with red hair.

Some women call me their special rider, some ladies call me their sugar candy man.
Some women think I'm a special rider, Lord, some ladies call me the sugar candy man.

To some women, I'm the dirty old drunk at the end of the frying pan.

There are footprints in the sand, sister, but they've left me with nothin' I can use.

There ain't no one carryin' me, except the blacker shade of the blues.

Blacker Shade Of Blue

Fingers Flaherty

Chapter 9

Blue Suede Eyes

I woke up this morning under a strange blue sun,
On another planet's soil, gripping a hot shotgun,
Wondering what the hell I did before last night was done.
Guess what I saw when I opened up my eyes!
Little planet Earth shooting straight across the skies.
I rolled over on the pillow and it just told me more lies.

Blinded By The Blues
Fingers Flaherty

Groaning himself awake, Moses was amazed to discover that, although he felt distinctly groggy and his mouth tasted like the death of an empire, he did not have a hangover.

Saoirse had got a taxi home after they left the Skulldiggery. They had considered ordering a taxi, ambulance or hearse for Banjo, but he had suddenly tapped into some secret energy source and disappeared into the night, searching for the twenty-four-hour twelve-bar blues club he had read about in *Dublin Swings*. And searching for Rita too. Saoirse later told Moses that Rita had been proactively celibate since her last encounter with Banjo.

Moses had tried to convince Saoirse to head back to his apartment. He needed that assurance that their budding relationship was back on the tracks. She insisted that she felt drunk and tired and wanted to head home alone. He kissed her as she got into the taxi and walked home, trying to work out what skeletons were currently driving the relationship.

Staring up at the ceiling in the warm, curtained light of a lazy Sunday morning, he knew that he still didn't have a clue. Part of him thought that he'd never have a clue and that he should just gladly accept his ignorance.

His mobile phone started ringing.

Moses's hand fumbled along the floor looking for his jeans. He finally located them and fished out the phone.

"Hello?"

Moses then could hear breathing.

Slow, heavy breathing.

"Come on! Quit playing games."

For one terrified second, Moses wondered if the heavy breather was the lovesick skinhead from the Skulldiggery.

"I'm going to hang up now!"

The breathing began to slow down.

"Moses, it's me," a familiar voice gasped. "I'm shattered."

"Floyd?" Moses wanted to strangle the squirrel. "What the hell are you playing at, you mad bastard?"

"I'm out of breath, Moses." The squirrel's voice was getting steadier. "I'm escaping from them."

"Who? Are you in some sort of trouble?"

"No, I just like sprinting for my life first thing on a Sunday morning," Floyd snapped. "This is serious shit. They're going to kill me. I hope this lamppost hides me from –"

"Who?" Moses could feel a headache beginning to get dressed in his head. "What? Why?"

"The Elvis Appreciation Chapter. I think they want to assassinate me. Because of the stupid clambake!"

"I see." Moses reached out for his pack of cigarettes, hoping a shot of nicotine would blast away the morning cobwebs. "Could you perhaps elaborate?"

"I was at our Sunday morning worship service and Victor, the head of our chapter, was giving a sermon about *Clambake*, Elvis's 1967 movie. Have you ever seen it?"

"Of course I haven't!"

"Good. Never try to watch it. You'd have more fun pouring warm acid into your eyes."

"I thought you adored Elvis." Moses blew a cloud of smoke to the ceiling. "What's wrong with the movie?"

"Even fans have their limits, Moses. And *Clambake* is mine. It involves speedboat racing, beach balls, water skiing and oil barons. Do I really need to explain any further? I started laughing at the sermon. I thought Victor was joking when he called the movie a 'neo-Renaissance absurdist masterpiece'. The movie was nearly as absurd as Victor's jumpsuit. Believe me, certain men were born to never wear a jumpsuit! But the other folks in the chapter didn't appreciate my heresy. Now they want to turn me into a modern Joan of Arc!"

"Ah, the rare medium who ended up well done!" Moses's laughter caused his brain to rattle inside his skull.

"I'm about to get roasted alive and all you can do is make terrible jokes?"

Moses stretched himself in his bed. The squirrel's trauma made him appreciate the bed's warmth and comfort even more.

"Anyway, Moses, I think I'm safe from the mob for now. I was ringing to find out how last night went."

"Okay, I think." *Actually, I haven't a fucking clue.* "Banjo was in usual order. Comatose and incoherent. And Saoirse was... Saoirse seemed to be in good form... I think..."

"How did *you* enjoy the night?" The squirrel sounded anxious. "Don't be alarmed if I have to abandon this conversation without warning. The Elvis Assassination Squad is liable to appear with burning love and burning oil at any time. They like taking care of business. However, I should be fairly safe up here, sitting on this lamppost on the corner of the street."

"I think it was a good night, Floyd." Moses rubbed his eyes, shielding them from the smoke. "Banjo was as drunk as an electrocuted monkey, needless to say. But I think Saoirse and I are back on the tracks. Some sort of tracks anyway. Even if I'm not sure where exactly they lead to. Every day is at the mercy of a simple twist of fate."

"That's sounds hopeful. And probably blindly optimistic."

"I thought I saw Natalie in the Skulldiggery." Moses was aware of a stronger smell of smoke. "But it wasn't her."

"Moses, you're pining for the soup while you're eating the main course. Talk about being unable to focus on the pressing issues! It's a good job you weren't organising the original exodus. They'd all be back building pyramids before they knew what happened to them. You need to say goodbye to all that. I know 'Goodbye' is the hardest word in the language."

"I usually have trouble with 'Hello'!" The smoke was causing

Moses's eyes to water. "I can't help still having feelings for Natalie. Those feelings have started making themselves known again ever since Saoirse started acting… odd this last few days."

"You're turning Natalie into some great mythic goddess of the past. We should probably meet up later to discuss this further. I'll bring my beard and analyst's couch with me."

"I could get Saoirse to write a thesis on her," Moses muttered sourly. The bed now felt too warm. "And maybe get Fingers Flaherty to write a poison ballad about her."

"Remember what I said to you soon after we met. Natalie is still the key, Moses. What you have to realise is… Shit!" Floyd uttered a panic-stricken yelp. "The Elvis mafia are coming. And they're carrying blowtorches. They must want to roast my nuts. I'll meet you later and we can finish our analysis of all that's wrong with you."

The squirrel hung up before Moses could respond.

The room now seemed to be shimmering in a warm cloud of smoke. Moses dozed there, sweating, idly planning the rest of his day.

Maybe I'll just lie here all day, sweating and dreaming.

Moses suddenly realised why the bed was so hot.

Some cigarette ash had fallen on the sheets.

Fuck it! Guess I'll have to get up.

Moses saw that the sheets were on fire.

The king is in his counting house, counting all his money.
Queen Bee is on her feather bed, licking up the honey.
God is laughing up there, but His joke ain't that funny.
Guess what I saw under the emperor's fine clothes!

A skeleton snorting handfuls of dust up its nose,
Wearing a jester's mask to the carnival shows.

Blinded By The Blues
Fingers Flaherty

After mass, Moses headed into town. He decided to go the Maestro Bistro for lunch. It was one of those hyper-trendy bistros where beautiful people had beautiful conversations while enjoying beautiful meals at not so beautiful prices. Like many places in Dublin, it tried to recreate the existential chic of French coffee houses. However, the only thing Parisian about Maestro Bistro was the attitude of the waiters, who tended to regarded customers as dog turds on the manicured boulevards of their lives.

On the way, Moses met Paul and invited him to join him. Kate Bush's "King Of The Mountain" played ever so discreetly on the speakers as they entered. They found a table and settled down for their lunch.

Moses was still trying to come to terms with how relaxed and breezy Paul looked in his loose, open-necked cream shirt and white slacks. His clean-shaven face shone fresh and rested. Moses could barely believe that this was the same Paul who slouched beside him at work. Maybe he was in disguise.

Fr Pepper's sermon was still scurrying inside Moses's head. The theme today had been masks. Fr Pepper talked about how everyone wore a disguise. People were not always even aware that they were wearing disguises. However, Pepper argued, Jesus could see through the disguise.

"He can see the innocent woman beneath the prostitute's disguise," Pepper had said. "He can see the frightened sinner quivering beneath the tax collector's mask. Jesus pierced through these social veils and saw the spiritually rich woman inside the poor widow."

Moses ordered the soup and turkey and ham, and Paul went for the fruit salad and steak. U2's "Elvis Ate America" began clattering in the background.

"Paul, can I ask you something?"

"Sure."

"Well, if you don't mind me asking, have you gone through some sort of… um… reincarnation this weekend? You seem more… at peace than I've ever known you. And you're looking very sharp today. You usually look like something decomposing in a ditch. With a face that only a blind man would paint."

"Oh, that." Paul laughed. "We all loosen the bolts a bit at the weekend."

"I know. But… well, you're always such a relentlessly miserable bastard at work. We usually lose two hours of sunshine when you walk into a room."

"Thanks a lot." Paul did not sound in the least bit offended. "That office would depress Laughie the Happy Clown from Sunshine Valley. The job is meaningless beyond a suicidal existentialist's worst nightmare. But once I get back out into normal humanity again, I'm fine because I can relax and enjoy myself. Then back on Monday, it's time to sink into despair again. Face it, you'd need to be a self-delusional maniac not to be sceptical in that place!"

"It's a way of dealing with it." *I wish I was able to relax and enjoy myself!* "Did you get up to anything last night?"

"Not really." Paul shrugged. "A quiet night in with a six pack and a few DVDs. I can't burn it at both ends every weekend. And you?"

"Pretty good. I went to the Skulldiggery with Saoirse and Banjo. I accidentally felt up some skinhead guy, but apart from that, the night was relatively free from trauma."

They sat in silence for some moments. Soon the waiter slid by with the starters.

"This morning has been a bit of a disaster," Moses said, after a few spoons of soup. "I set the bed on fire."

"Moses," Paul said, holding up his hand. "I'm really glad that you and Saoirse are getting on well, but spare me the details."

"Not like that." Moses laughed. "I was on my own."

"Own your own? Jesus, you must have been going at it like a jackhammer. I suppose enough static friction would generate sparks and –"

"A stupid cigarette set the sheets on fire. That's all."

"Oh, I see. What did you do?"

"Well, I turned over and got another forty winks because the bed was so cosy. What the hell do you think I did? I went into the kitchen and got a glass of water."

"Did that help?"

"It would have." Moses grimaced at the memory. "Unfortunately, my throat was parched from all the smoke. I drank the water on my way back to the bedroom. I was so fucking thirsty, I forgot about the fire!"

Elvis Costello's "Chelsea" began playing when the waiter brought the main courses. They ate in silence, savouring the food.

"Did you know," Moses asked, chewing on some ham, "that El Coconut has the hots for Lydia?"

"Get away! He's incapable of experiencing human emotions. They left that chip on the factory floor when they built him."

"That's what I would have thought." Moses nodded, hoping the movement would help the piece of ham finally complete the journey down his throat. "He got totally pissed in the office on Friday evening and started asking me all these questions about her. Just goes to show how you can never fully know a person."

"Even coconuts know how to cry," Paul said with mock gravitas, steak juice dribbling down the side of his chin. "Very touching."

"He also told me that he wanted to shove a white-hot cattle prod up your arse. You'd better be on the lookout! You never know when he'll decide to have a cull."

"Well, if taking part in Fred's kinky games is what's needed to optimise my leveraged resources, I suppose I'll have to rise to the challenge and bring my arse to the table. I'd better put in a purchase requisition order for a new chair at work."

They drifted back into their private worlds. Moses wondered what Fr Pepper would make of Fred. Beneath Fred's rough, hard exterior, it appeared that there was a soft centre. Weakness hidden behind a hairy mask.

Paul and Moses idly chattered about work through the rest of the meal. They watched the rude waiter insult a variety of customers and some of his colleagues. Moses recounted memories of his first awful weeks in Aztech. Paul tried, unsuccessfully, to envisage a career path for himself within the company. They both agreed there'd be too many landmines in that path.

The coffees arrived. Moses was feeling good. The talk with Paul had cheered him up. It took his mind off Saoirse. And Natalie.

Alannah Myles sang "Black Velvet" in the background.

"So how exactly are things between you and Saoirse?" Paul asked. "Will you be able to pay some attention to your work next week?"

"As far as I know." Moses shrugged. "It's… complicated."

"That's what makes it interesting, I suppose. And as annoying as a paper cut."

"Charming image, Paul. 'My love is as annoying as a paper cut.' Shakespeare would have given three of his fingers for a line like that. Anyway, I think me and Saoirse will manage to stumble through this fog somehow. We haven't scaled the heights of absurdity that my neighbours have reached."

"What are they up to?" Paul finished his coffee. "Or do I want to know? Does it involve cattle prods?"

"They are trying to bring their dressy-uppy role-playing sex games to a new level."

"That can least at liven up the dull moments." A mischievous smile spread across Paul's face. "Do you think Saoirse would be on for dressing up, Moses?"

Moses didn't answer. He stared into the depths of his coffee, slightly shaken.

What the fuck is wrong with my head?

As soon as Paul mentioned about Saoirse in disguise, Moses had seen the image.

Saoirse standing in the bedroom. In disguise. Smiling at him. Blowing kisses at him, flirting shamelessly.

Wearing a red wig. Dressed up as Natalie.

"That was nice coffee." Moses hoped he could derail the conversation. "Let's get the bill before the waiter gets fired."

I saw her standing there, Lord, a blazing beauty to his beast.
The devil stirred inside me, Lord, I'd better go find a priest.
The graves threw up their dead, as the memories were released.
Guess what I saw when I gazed into her face!
The ghost of Christmas past, packing up my suitcase.
I know I left my heart lying around here some place.

Blinded By The Blues
Fingers Flaherty

The phone was ringing when Moses walked back into his apartment.

"Hello?" *I wonder if Floyd is in trouble again.* "Who's this?"

"Moses, it's Stephen."

"Oh!" Moses was in no mood to talk to his brother. "What do you want?"

"Nothing much."

"What did you ring for, then?" *Something's up!* "Goodbye."

"Did you meet Dad for lunch today, Moses?"

"No. We made other plans. He said he was busy these days."

"He's busy a lot lately." Stephen's voice sounded strained. "Hardly has time to finish a conversation. Always rushing off before –"

"Anyway, I'll be talking to you again some –"

"Moses, do you think… I was just wondering if… I don't know."

"Wondering what?" Moses could feel himself getting sucked into conversational quicksand. "What are you talking about?"

"Do you think he has… maybe… formed a relationship?"

"Relationship?"

"Do you think he has started… you know… going out with someone?" Stephen now sounded embarrassed. "Has he said anything to you?"

"Are you insane? Why would he bother after all these years?"

"For God's sake, Moses," Stephen snapped, "he's not in the coffin yet! He still has a few hands to play."

"Don't let your imagination run away with itself." Moses didn't want to admit that the same question had been gnawing at him. He had enough to worry about without discussing the stepmother complex with his brother. "I'm sure he's just… busy."

"Maybe." Stephen sighed, sounding utterly unconvinced. "Anyway, how are things with you?"

"Great. Smashing. Super."

"I'm keeping well, too. Thanks for asking."

"That's just wonderful, Stephen." *Time to bail out of this conversation. I'm not becoming his surrogate father.* "I just assumed that you'd be keeping well. After all, nothing bad ever happens to you."

"Do you want to meet up for a few drinks tonight?"

"No, I'll be busy. We can do it again some time soon."

Moses hung up before Stephen could interrupt him. He went into his bedroom and turned on the Flaherty CD. He lay on the new bed sheets, trying not to imagine his father's romantic adventures.

He closed his eyes as the opening strums of "Look What Ya Gone And Done" filled the room. Flaherty's twenty-verse tale of a romantic encounter with geriatric twin sisters at a Gamblers' Anonymous meeting was easier to deal with.

Someone's laughing, Lord, and I think it's at me.
Someone's crying, Lord, they've seen what I see.
Someone's praying, Lord, for the bride to be.
Guess what I saw when I walked into the room!
Alice and the cat talking to the mushroom,
Singing 'Kumbaya' to lighten the gloom.

Blinded By The Blues
Fingers Flaherty

At 6.00, Moses headed toward St Paul's Park. Floyd had insisted that they needed to continue their therapy session.

Walking out of Ellington Court, Moses met Bill, who was carrying a sports bag.

"Hello, Bill. On your way back from the gym?"

"Gym?" Bill blinked at Moses. "What on earth makes you think that?"

"The sports bag was the first clue, my dear Watson. Also, the tea leaf melted half an inch into the butter. Between all that and the fact that the dog didn't bark, it was an elementary deduction. Eliminate all other possibilities and whatever remains must be true, no matter how absurd."

"Oh, this!" Bill held up the sports bag. "My life may be in chaos, Moses, but I haven't yet resorted to going to the gym to find some meaning for it all. It's my costume."

"Costume? Are you going to a fancy-dress party?"

"No, not really. " Bill looked flustered, and began glancing up and down Shaw Road. "It's more a… uniform."

"Uniform?" Moses enjoyed seeing Bill get more uncomfortable. Tonight was obviously the night for the latest role-playing experiment. "Since when have office supply salesmen had to wear uniforms?"

"No, it's not for work. It's… recreational."

"I see." Moses had to chew his tongue to keep from smiling. "Sounds like fun."

"It should be… Hopefully… Anyway, enough of this aimless bullshitting. I'd better head on in."

Bill went into Ellington Court, clutching his sports bag.

St Paul's Park was emptying out as the day's heat began to fade. Some young boys were playing football. Some couples walked around, holding hands and smiling into each other's eyes. Others couples sat on the grass, glaring at each other in silence.

Floyd was lying stretched out near the lake wearing his Sunday best: white Panama hat, navy blue sports jacket, dazzling white shirt and crisp tan slacks. The sun glistened on his patent leather shoes. Expensive sunglasses protected the squirrel from the glare.

Floyd was smoking a cigarillo, gazing at the ducks.

"How are you, Floyd?"

"Sweet and easy. I've just been idling here the last half-hour, looking at the ducks. How has your day been? Any burning issues?"

"You could say that. I accidentally dropped some cigarette ash on the bed sheets and nearly set fire to the entire fucking building."

Moses gazed at the ducks in the centre of the lake as Floyd slowly worked his way through a guffaw.

"I can't seem to figure out Saoirse these days." Moses sighed. "She seems to be broadcasting from another planet. Or maybe I am."

"Observe how by carefully extinguishing any embers I can prevent the grass catching fire." Floyd stubbed out his cigarillo. "It's a basic precaution to take with any form of cigarette."

"That's just great advice, Dr Floyd!" Moses glared at the squirrel. "I'm glad I don't pay you on an hourly basis."

Floyd seemed to be obsessed with making sure his cigarillo was extinguished. He stood up and jumped on the ashes a few times, spitting on any smoking remains. Moses watched the bizarre pantomime and then concentrated on the less demanding scene of the ducks aimlessly meandering in the lake.

"The ducks seem to be having a good day," he observed. "They seem to be as content as… as a duck has any right to expect to be."

"They *seem* to be happy." Floyd was now scrutinising his shoes, making sure no grass or ash had robbed them of their sheen. "Of course, they're paddling like bastards under the water. All calm on the surface, all chaos beneath. You shouldn't really be taking them as role models, Moses."

"What do you suggest then?" Moses looked down at the squirrel. "And stop doing whatever the hell it is you are doing. It's beginning to get on my nerves!"

"I'm just making sure I haven't dirtied my shoes with the cigarillo."

Floyd was now shaking some ash out of his tail. "The ash gets everywhere. I didn't get all dressed up just to coat myself in ash."

"Smoked cigarillo is soon forgotten." Moses sighed. "Unless you happen to be a fastidious squirrel. Anyway, I've got your message. Don't leave smouldering cigarettes lying around, or else I might set fire to myself. That's today's public service announcement."

Moses looked at the ducks, wondering if they could help him understand life.

The ducks looked back at him, serene and smug.

"I'm meeting Saoirse in about an hour, Floyd. I'm terrified that she's going to give me the elbow. Or the cold shoulder."

"Why doesn't she just give you the whole arm and be done with it? The key thing to remember is that if you don't carefully extinguish your cigarettes, you might set your bed on fire."

Moses resisted the temptation to kick the squirrel into the lake. He took his frustration out on a few innocent blades of grass, tearing them from the soil.

"I can see that I haven't got through to you, Moses," the squirrel said. "Don't tie yourself into knots over this. Unless that's what you're into."

"So I should just do nothing? You've surpassed yourself, Floyd!"

"I've got to go." Floyd carefully straightened the hat on his head. "I have to meet the Elvis Inquisition down at the club and explain my recent lapse. I'll drop into Ellington Court later on."

"I'll try and get some sense out of Saoirse this evening."

"You do that, Moses." Floyd checked his watch and started walking off. "And don't accidentally leave things smouldering around the place."

Moses gazed at the retreating squirrel. In the background, a duck quacked.

That didn't shed any light on Moses's dilemma.

After wandering around the park, completely lost in fruitless thought, for twenty minutes, Moses heard someone calling him.

"Moses? How are you?"

It's not her, is it?

He turned around, slowly, both nervous and excited.

"Hello, stranger." She smiled. "I'd recognise that world-weary slouch anywhere!"

"Hello, Natalie," Moses mumbled. "How are you?"

The first thing, the *only* thing, Moses noticed was that she looked stunning. She wore light blue jeans, a green top and a denim jacket. Her hair was cut shorter than Moses remembered it, making it a darker shade of red, making her face seem brighter.

She took off her sunglasses and scrutinised him, smiling.

"I'm good, Moses. How are you?"

"Good," Moses lied. "Things are going… great, in some ways."

Christ almighty, she looks even better than I remember! She was never this carefree and… relaxed. She hardly ever used to wear casual clothes. Has it been only a few months since we split up? Jesus, it seems like a lifetime away.

"You look tired, Moses. Is work still getting you down?"

"Not really. Actually, it's going quite well. That performance review a while back was a bit of a farcical disaster, but –"

"Why was that?" Natalie sounded genuinely interested. And concerned. "Any particular reason? You're not going to get fired, are you?"

"I don't think so. It was just a personality clash, I suppose." *I couldn't stop thinking about you during the review.* "But things improved as time went on."

Christ, what were all those things I promised I'd say to her if we ever met again? All those things I wanted to explain.

"So… Natalie… how is life treating you?"

"Things are fine. The promotion is working out great, so I'm enjoying the job more. And the holiday to Spain with Jenny and Elizabeth took years off me. I came back totally refreshed, ready to start things over."

"How is Tony Lyons keeping?" *Is that big, long, lanky, bandy-legged, ugly rake of a thing still burning your bed sheets?* "Are you two still… um… an item?"

"No." For the first time, Natalie's smile faltered. She cast her eyes down. "In the end, things didn't work out… He wasn't the guy I thought he'd be. Guess I backed the wrong donkey. As per! The disguise falls away and it's not pleasant underneath."

Disguise? Is everyone role playing these days?

"I'm not in disguise, Natalie." The attempted laugh got lost somewhere in his throat. "Not everyone wears a disguise."

"I know that, Moses." She put back on her sunglasses. "I think I learned a long time ago how to see through any of your disguises."

"It wasn't all bad." *Jesus Christ, why I am straying into this?* "There were some good times."

"Yes." Natalie nodded, smiling briefly. "Some… brief happy memories."

"Like that night we went for a meal in Pepperpot's and then spent hours just walking around the city, talking about absolutely nothing. It was a freezing February night and the stars were –"

"I remember. There are some memories like that."

It was so cold that we could see our breath in front of us. You leaned into me as we walked, trying to keep each other warm. I wanted to walk with you forever that night. We shared memories. You told me about your primary school teacher who looked like Jimmy Carter. He used to make you stand at the back of the class. And I told you about the Christmas a few years ago when Dad burnt the dinner to an atomic crisp. He had to get us an un-Christian take-away instead. And we enjoyed that take-away more than any other meal that year.

Natalie began to look slightly uncomfortable. She glanced at her watch.

"Would you like to meet for a drink some time?" Moses asked before she could say anything. "Give us time to catch up on all that has happened."

"I don't know, Moses." She frowned. "It might be best to wait a while."

You were wearing that new white jacket. You complained that it couldn't keep you warm. You laughed when I gave you my suede jacket. I had a bastard of a cold for a week after that, and you called around every evening to see if I had recovered.

Moses looked around the park. There were hardly any people left. The young boys were heading home, their game of football finished. A young couple were kissing, almost hidden in the shade of a tree. An old man was walking his dog.

"I don't mean that we should go for a drink this evening," Moses said, determined not to let the opportunity completely pass. "Maybe we could meet up later this week. I've already got plans for this evening."

"Perhaps." Natalie shrugged. "What are you doing this evening?"

"I'm... meeting Jesse and Lucy for a meal."

"Oh, how is Jesse?" Natalie broke into a smile. "I haven't been talking to him since... well, in ages."

"He's keeping well, it seems. He and Lucy have become very friendly. Something of an item, almost."

"Really?" Natalie laughed, obviously delighted. "Poor old Jesse needed someone to take his mind off mouldy old blues singers."

"He's still mad about Fingers. I suppose you can't expect him to forget about his idol just because... his life has taken a few new turns."

Or was it Ronald Reagan your teacher looked like? He sounded like a complete bastard, anyway. I remember how angry you got as you talked about him, your voice trembling in the breeze. I told you that it was all in the past, that he couldn't make fun of you any more.

"I'd better go." Natalie glanced at her watch again. "Time flies by and the evening's gone before you know what has happened."

"Yes, time does tend to shoot by when... Anyway, you have my number if you change your mind about meeting up for a drink."

"Bye, Moses." Natalie gently hugged him and kissed him lightly on the cheek. "It was good to see you again."

"It was great to talk to you, Natalie." Her perfume engulfed him for some seconds. He expected to have a heart attack at any moment. "Perhaps we'll be in touch soon."

Natalie was already walking away. He could still smell her perfume. He wanted to stay standing there.

Then he remembered that Saoirse would be calling around in half an hour.

"I thought that was a lovely sermon Fr Pepper gave this morning," Lucy said, as they sat down in the sitting room of Jesse's apartment. Dean Martin's "Volare" played on the stereo. "Sometimes he can get straight to the bone of an issue."

"Really?" Saoirse glanced at Moses, apparently surprised that the Sunday sermon was considered a viable topic of conversation. "What was he talking about?"

"Pepper talks as if he thinks his words are being recorded for posterity," Jesse said with a laugh. "He was talking this morning about seeing into people."

Moses saw that Saoirse seemed to be in a good mood, relaxing easily with Jesse and Lucy. She was dressed in black trousers and a light-blue blouse, more formal than usual. She had presented Jesse with a bottle of wine when they arrived.

"He spoke about how we should always look beneath the surface of people," Lucy continued, pouring some more wine. She glanced over at Jesse. "People are rarely as they first appear. Take my niece Bubbles. I'm sorry to tell you, Moses, that she has met someone new."

Moses felt a surge of relief charge through him.

"She's been going out with a nice young man from her volunteer group," Lucy continued. "Their eyes met while they were feeding the homeless by the canal. I do hope the young man doesn't end up homeless. Bubbles can have a strange effect on people... Anyway, my point is that Bubbles is a completely new person now. Somewhere beneath all that screaming anger, there was a romantic princess waiting to be freed. With any luck, the police won't get dragged into her romantic endeavours this time."

"That's what makes life interesting!" Jesse smiled back. "Boring people live on the surface. They have no secrets to reveal. Interesting people reveal something new every day."

"Yes," Lucy said. "You could be wearing a disguise and not know it."

"Disguise?" Moses jerked forward. "Who's wearing disguises?"

Paul Simon began crooning "Still Crazy After All These Years". The song made Lucy smile wistfully.

"Are you alright, Moses?" Saoirse turned to him, concern and puzzlement fighting for expression. "You've been... on edge all evening."

"I'm fine." Moses shrugged. "Not a thing wrong with me. Nothing at all. Everything is absolutely –"

"Saoirse, how did you meet Moses?" Jesse asked. "Were you perhaps doing some social work down in the asylum?"

"Actually," Saoirse said, smiling into her glass of wine, "I met him in a jungle."

"I see." Lucy's eyebrows shot up. "Do you often visit the jungle?"

"Not literally." Saoirse laughed. "It was a club in town called Halogen. I met Moses swinging from a vine. I think the music was a bit too manic for him. But we got talking and… one thing led to… another."

"And another thing led to another." Moses smiled, remembering the walk home that night. "We just keep bumping into each other ever since."

They drank in silence for some minutes, as Paul Simon declared that he wouldn't be convicted by a jury of his peers.

"So we've sort of decided to continue the experiment," Saoirse said, gently squeezing Moses's hand, "and try not to blow up the laboratory."

"Yes." *Why did she squeeze my hand? Think of something sensible to say!* "On into the future, away from the past. Put out all the embers."

They all stared at Moses, slightly puzzled. Even Paul Simon sounded confused.

"To the future," Moses said, raising his glass. "Let's toast the future."

A slightly bewildered toast ensued.

"It has been… an eventful few weeks," Moses said after some minutes, deciding that his toast deserved further elaboration. "We've all put a few things behind us and… have moved on… to… better things."

"Really, Moses!" Saoirse exploded into laughter. "You are beginning to sound like an unhinged life coach. Next you'll be saying that we need a new bottle of wine for a new evening."

"It's just that it's good to…" Moses realised, with a sinking feeling, that he was blushing. "We need to put the past few weeks behind us."

"I hear you're working on a thesis, Saoirse." Lucy obviously felt that Moses couldn't be relied on to navigate the conversation. "How's that coming along?"

"It has good days and bad days." Saoirse shrugged. "But it seems to be getting there."

A commotion erupted in the main hallway. Footsteps were loudly pounding down the stairs.

"You sick-headed bastard!" Tiffany's voice yelled down the stairs, chasing the footsteps. "You need professional fucking help!"

"You said that you were into it," Bill's voice wailed back up the stairs. "You said you wanted to role play again in the privacy of our own lovely home."

"You should be rolled into a car crusher!" Tiffany's voice was gaining power. "I'll help you on your way."

Everyone in the room glanced at each other as the exchange faded.

"Anyway," said Jesse, standing up, "I'd better go into the kitchen and see if the food is ready. You can all sort yourselves out around the table."

Everyone stood up and began deciding the seating arrangements.

"Good God almighty!" Jesse exclaimed from the kitchen. "What on earth is going on in the car park?"

They rushed in to the kitchen.

Jesse was staring out the window in disbelief.

They squeezed around Jesse, craning their necks to see the scene in the car park.

"My God," Lucy whispered.

"What's going on?" Saoirse asked.

"This takes the biscuit," Moses whispered, "and lets it eat cake."

In the car park, an argument was in full swing. Two people were shouting at each other, their voices carrying over to Jesse's window.

To the right stood a woman dressed as a nurse. She was shouting, pointing accusingly at the other person. Her hand trembled with rage.

The woman was obviously Tiffany.

The other person was Donald Duck.

Donald threw his arms up in the air, trying to explain himself. The costume was remarkably detailed, from the yellow legs up to the sailor's hat on top of the duck's mask. The louder the nurse shouted, the more the duck jumped up and down, protesting his innocence.

The man beneath the duck's costume was Bill.

"Role playing," Moses explained to the others, as they continued to stare out the window. "It helps… warm up relationships, apparently."

"Couldn't they have come up with something more… conventional?" Jesse shook his head. "Donald Duck and a nurse. Astounding!"

"They really do have problems." Lucy sounded sad. "God only knows how this display is going to help them."

"Ducks are very complex creatures," Moses said. "All calm on the surface, but mad chaos going on beneath it all."

"I wouldn't like to know what is going on beneath the surface of that," Jesse said, pointing at the car park. "Freud would have a great time with them."

"Have you no idea how sick you are?" Tiffany yelled at Donald Duck, her fury reaching an impressive crescendo. "I agreed to a bit of fun. I did not agree to this. Walt Disney would turn in his grave."

"He's actually in a cryogenic chamber," Donald Duck pointed out.

"I don't care if he's in a camel's arse!"

"I thought you told me to dress up as a duck." Bill took off the mask and stared at her, a picture of baffled innocence. "I assumed that you were going to dress up as Daisy Duck. Or maybe Minnie Mouse."

"I told you get a doctor's outfit!"

"Oh." The light began to dawn in Bill's eyes. "Doctor... Not duck."

"Exactly!" Tiffany stormed towards him and grabbed him by his feathery shoulders. "Doctors and nurses. That was as far as I was prepared to go with this role-playing shite. Thank God I insisted we keep this experiment private!"

"You make a pretty nurse." Bill grinned at her. "Can you heal me?"

"How the fuck can I heal someone who dresses up as Donald Duck in order to seduce me?"

"I don't know," Bill said in a Donald Duck voice. "Are you mad at me, Daisy?"

"Good God!" Tiffany shook her head in disbelief. "You should be shot and served with gravy."

"Mickey and Minnie sorted out their problems," the Donald Duck voice continued. "Can't we still be friends? I want to be your friend, Daisy."

"What can I say?" Tiffany glared at him. "Give me one good reason why I shouldn't seal you up in a sewer."

"Because I'm me." Donald Duck scratched his head. "Let me see. How about this?"

Bill took a harmonica out of the inside pocket of the sailor suit.

"This is for you, Daisy," he said, still in his Donald Duck voice.

Bill started blowing into the harmonica. Slowly, an extremely shaky version of "My Way" began to emerge. In the silence of the car park, the harmonica notes wailed, timid at first, then with growing confidence.

"I actually think Freud would be out of his depth," Jesse remarked, looking at the bizarre serenade. "Anyone would be."

Tiffany watched Bill's performance in disbelief. Her fury seemed to slightly wane when Bill began an exaggerated shuffle dance to accompany his increasingly frenzied harmonica playing. His yellow legs shot up and down as he wriggled his feathery hips, trying to develop some obscure variation of Chuck Berry's duck-walk dance routine.

Every few seconds, Bill lost his breath and his face began to turn an intriguing shade of purple-green. The harmonica seemed to be trying to escape from his wheezing lips.

Tiffany looked like she was waiting for Bill to swallow the harmonica. She let the performance continue for some minutes before her facade cracked and she started laughing. This encouraged Bill to exaggerate his dance routine outrageously. Soon, tears of laughter were rolling down Tiffany's face.

"Bill certainly seems to know the way to Tiffany's heart." Lucy smiled, as Tiffany threw her arms around the dancing Donald Duck. "He just seems to get severely lost along the way."

The nurse and Donald Duck were now waltzing around the car

park.

Bill, you always put things into perspective. I'm still a million miles away from your problems. I think…

The nurse let out a startled yell when Donald Duck suddenly swept her off her feet. Still continuing the duck-walk dance, Donald Duck carried the nurse into Ellington House.

"Anyway," Jesse said, shaking his bemused gaze away from the car park, "we didn't come here to watch… that. Let's get the food going."

Ten minutes later, they were all sitting around the table in Jesse's sitting room. The food was set out before them: hamburgers, chips and side salad. Another bottle of wine was opened.

The Beatles' "Help" played as the conversation ambled through various subjects, including the continuing hot weather, the recent government collapse, the new soap opera on RTÉ and the difficulties facing students in modern Dublin.

Moses tried to stay focused on the conversation, but his mind kept breaking free from its chain. He hoped his face looked calmer than he felt.

He was turning over what Natalie had said in the park. Her talk about disguises. She hadn't sounded angry, but he felt that she had accused him of something. And whenever he made eye contact with Saoirse, he saw a shadow of the same accusation flicker in her eyes.

"Don't you agree, Moses?" Jesse asked.

"What?" *Fuck! What are we talking about now? Is that John Lennon singing?* "I'm sorry… I… um… lost the train of the discussion."

"I was just saying," Jesse said, with a hint of impatience, "that every person you get to know has an effect on you some way."

"Oh, sure." *A squirrel with an interesting name had a profound influence on my life. So did a dead blues-singing alcoholic.* "That's why we are always trying to meet new people. For example, I think my father has met someone new."

"Really?" Jesse leaned forward, intrigued. "I thought you said he was never going to get married again."

"I'm not talking about bloody marriage! I'm just saying that he seems to have met someone new."

"And how do you feel about that?" Jesse asked.

"Fine," Moses lied, wondering why he had strolled into this emotional minefield. "He seems... happier. Which makes my life easier. And his as well, I suppose."

"If he has found someone special," Jesse said, smiling at Lucy, "he certainly will feel happier."

"I suppose so," Moses admitted, remembering how he'd felt when he left Halogen that night. "Although I think he's only happy when he's angry, if that's not a contradiction."

"We all have our contradictions to deal with," Saoirse said, drinking her wine. "Life is never as black and white as it first appears."

"There are plenty of contradictions," Moses agreed. "There seems to be chaos under the surface, no matter where you look."

"It's not chaos." Jesse smiled. "It's just interesting."

"That display in the car park," Lucy laughed, "proves that life is anything but boring."

Once the food was finished, Jesse and Lucy retreated to the kitchen to prepare the coffee. On the stereo, "Do You Want To Dance?" by Bobby Freeman kicked off.

"They seem very happy together." Saoirse nodded towards the kitchen.

"Yes, they do. They both have plenty of baggage, but they seem to be working through it."

"Baggage is always a problem." Saoirse gazed into her wine glass, getting lost in thought. "It's how we deal with it that matters."

"Sure." *What the fuck is she talking about now?* "Remember that night in Halogen. When I danced over –"

"You were trying to dance, Moses," Saoirse pointed out, with a fleeting smile.

"Whatever. Anyway, remember there was some mad techno-rave shite blaring out of the speakers? Well, while I was dancing with you, I could hear that song. But in my head, I heard an orchestra playing Vivaldi's 'Spring'. We were dancing in a castle, a mansion, while the plague ravaged the country outside. Inside the walls, it was only us. I could hear that orchestra, even while that jungle shit was pounding my ears to death."

"Really?" Saoirse didn't seem to know how to respond. "Your imagination was obviously still quite… active."

"Yes, my mind was racing faster than that techno song." Moses squeezed her hand, drawing it towards him. His heart was thumping. "That was the best contradiction I've ever been in. Do you see?"

"Moses," Saoirse said, searching his face, "I haven't a notion what you are trying to say."

"In one ear, all I could was a techno rave-up from hell. In the other ear, all I could hear was an orchestra from another century playing classical music. And there I was, dancing with you in the middle of it all."

Saoirse smiled at him, a faint hint of relief flashing across her face.

"How many sugars do you take, Saoirse?" Jesse shouted from the kitchen.

"One," Saoirse called back, breaking her gaze with Moses. "And just a drop of milk."

Moses sat back, knowing that whatever spell had just enveloped them had now been broken. He took out a cigarette and lit up. His heartbeat began to slow back to a stable rhythm.

Moses gazed out the window at the trees in Ellington Court. He suddenly felt confused. He wasn't sure how much longer he could maintain this relatively calm facade.

Beneath the water, my feet are paddling like bastards.

He saw Floyd sitting on a branch. The squirrel smiled in at him.

"Saoirse, I'm going to head outside for a minute," he said, turning to her. "I feel a touch of a headache coming on. Tell Jesse and Lucy I'll be back in a minute."

Moses was out of the apartment before Saoirse could answer. As he walked to the main entrance, he could hear a harmonica softly playing in time to the bed springs in Bill and Tiffany's apartment upstairs.

Out in the courtyard, a discarded Donald Duck mask lay on the tarmac.

Moses went around to the back of the building and stood against the wall, making sure he couldn't be seen from Jesse's apartment. He stood there smoking.

"How's it hanging, Moses?" Floyd whispered, strolling around the corner. "Is the meal going well?"

"Yes," Moses answered. "It seems to be going just fine. How are you?"

"I was thinking about contradictions," Floyd answered. "And Elvis. You know, one year, Elvis sang 'Hound Dog' on national television and some people genuinely thought that he was possessed by the devil. He seemed to be that dangerous. That… unrepressed."

"Does this have anything to do with… anything?"

"Another year," Floyd continued, ignoring the interruption, "Elvis sang 'Amazing Grace' with a gospel quartet and meant every single word of it. On stage in the '70s, he could sing 'Teddy Bear' and 'How Great Thou Art' in the same concert. Anyone so intimately acquainted with God and the devil is bound to be interesting. Even if, at times, he seemed to be nothing more than a bloated fool lurching from one contradiction to the next."

Floyd had changed clothes since the park. He was now dressed in a dark-blue diamond-studded jumpsuit. He staggered slightly as he walked, a cigarillo dangling precariously from his lips. The effort of remaining upright was causing him to sweat heavily.

"Floyd, have you been drinking?"

"A few," the squirrel confessed. "After the Inquisition, we all decided to make up and get toasted, in a good way. We buried the hatchet and had a few celebratory bottles of tequila."

"Congratulations!" Moses threw his cigarette on the ground and stamped it out.

Floyd looked down at the crushed cigarette.

Moses could feel his tension disappear into the darkness.

"I met Natalie in the park today," he said, gazing into the sky. "She looked… great. It was… strange. I nearly fucking fainted when I saw her. Of course, my tongue turned to water. I can barely remember what I said to her."

"Must have been a fascinating conversation!"

"I know that part of me wanted to have sex with her right there in the park, with the ducks watching… Then she blew me out. I suggested that we meet up for drinks next week and she turned me down."

"That's hardly the end of the world, Moses."

"Maybe not." Moses shrugged. "The look in her eye when she turned me down reminded me of everything. It was the look she used to give me any time we were gearing up for a row. That look reminded me of every tedious argument we'd ever had. Arguments I had forgotten about. Big arguments about commitment and compromise and all that shite. Little arguments about the empty carton of milk and the unpaid broadband bill. Stupid arguments about politics and philosophy. Every single one of them has been replaying in my head all evening."

"Be careful your head doesn't explode." The squirrel laughed.

"Then tonight, I made eye contact with Saoirse and I could see her impatience with me. That barely repressed desire she had to grab the nearest wine bottle and smash it over my head."

"Your head really seems to be in danger," Floyd noted. "Maybe you should ask Nurse Tiffany if she has any bandages."

"In her eyes, I saw every argument we are going to have. All the serious ones and all the bullshit ones."

"Jesus, you really know how to liven up a party!"

"That's the thing, Floyd. It's not depressing." Moses nearly laughed out loud as he felt it all click into place. "I saw it all and I couldn't wait for it to get started. I wanted the good and the bad. All with Saoirse."

"I understand." Floyd smiled. "It looks like you've finally managed to stub all those cigarettes."

"What on earth," Moses sighed, "is your obsession with cigarettes these days? I am trying to explain my deepest feelings here."

"It's like this." Floyd began walking back and forth before Moses, waving his cigarillo for emphasis as he explained his theory. "You have been leaving smouldering cigarettes lying around behind you for months. And they eventually catch up with you and set off a fire. Your feelings for Natalie were the main problem, but there were plenty of smouldering cigarettes from work. You have gradually been stamping those out. Today, you stamped out the last one. Your feelings for Natalie are not going to catch fire again, because you finally understand them. You know it all has no more substance than a myth."

Moses watched the marching squirrel. Floyd was getting quite carried away with his explanation, looking like some lunatic professor trying to explain a radical re-interpretation of Shakespeare's sonnets. Or *Alice in Wonderland*.

"Your problem, Moses, was that you were always looking forward to some wild, exhilarating future that probably won't happen or else you were forever sighing nostalgically for some golden past that probably never really happened. You were biologically incapable of just being happy with the present."

"You should be carrying a placard," Moses laughed, "proclaiming:

'Floyd's Big Message'."

"You can laugh," Floyd said. "But it took you long enough to work out your feelings. I thought I was going to have to get a pair of pliers to untangle you at some stage."

"It's all about acceptance." Moses nodded. "Fr Pepper was right. You decide what you want and you accept it. You don't waste your time looking for miracles."

"Anyway, Moses, I have to go. I've got a big meeting in the morning and I don't want to fall asleep at it. I hope the rest of the evening goes well."

The squirrel started to walk away.

"Do you want to meet up for lunch tomorrow, Floyd?" Moses called out. "I can let you know how the evening worked out."

Floyd was already out of ear shot and continued to stumble away into the darkness, a trail of cigarillo smoke wafting behind him.

Moses checked his crushed cigarette to make sure it wasn't smouldering on the tarmac.

The harmonica was still gently playing as he walked into Ellington House.

When he walked back into Jesse's apartment, they were all sitting around the table, drinking coffee, discussing the new play that had opened in The Abbey.

Elvis Presley's "Burning Love" was playing on the stereo. Jesse seemed to be paying more attention to the song than to the conversation.

They all looked up when Moses walked in.

"Your coffee's probably gone cold," Lucy remarked. "You might need to boil a new cup."

Moses tasted the coffee and shuddered. It was stone cold.

"How does your head feel?" Saoirse asked him. "Is it better?"

"Yes," Moses smiled at her. "The fresh air cleared up my head completely."

He walked into the kitchen to make a new cup of hot coffee.

You wiggle like a snake, baby, you waddle like a duck.
The showband is really buzzing, better call the fire truck.
It's a poor man who has nothing if you take away his last buck.
Guess what I saw when I opened that door!
Just you and me, alone on that dark dance floor,
Gazing into each other's eyes until we could stand no more.

Blinded By The Blues
Fingers Flaherty

WRAPPING UP THE MUMMY

She walks like an Egyptian, her fingers poke my eyes,

Ancient secrets beneath her veil, legs of a goddess with human thighs.

She won't let me sleep at night, her ghost howls in my bedroom.

Once upon a time, I remember, I would have been glad to climb her

tower,

But that fire now has died, I no longer feel her power.

Now they're wrapping up the mummy, sealing up the tomb.

He sits in a bar with a brandy, a cigar and a whore.

He's got one eye on her skirt and one eye on the door.

She has his money in her pocket, she has his heart in her hands.

They woke up next morning in a strange deserted town,

He runs through the streets in her dirty dressing gown.

Now they're wrapping up the mummy, sweeping away the sands.

She's crossed that line, she's going down south,

So many teeth in such a pretty little mouth,

She chewed me up, she spat me out,

And wrapped me up without a doubt.

Pharaoh walks the desert looking for his queen, Jesus walks the hills

looking for a sinner,

She walks the bars looking for her husband, he walks the streets

looking for his dinner,

The senator is looking for his mistress, the shotgun bride is looking for her groom.

I can't remember what it was I'm supposed to be looking for,

I just follow her shadow through the bedroom door.

Now they're wrapping up the mummy, sealing up the tomb.

Acknowledgements

Thanks to the following for their advice and support:
Aidan Durkan, Anuwat Sangjindavong, Arlene Cunningham,
Bernadette Kenny, Chris Byrne, Colm McGee, David Campbell,
Declan Faughey, Declan Kiberd, Eamon Mag Uidhir, Eilish Hanratty,
Eleanor McNicholas, Emma Dunne, Helen McVeigh, John Webb,
Joyce Hickey, Karen Wiseman, Ken Drakeford, Kevin Stevens, Marie
Grant, Michéal Cunningham, Pat Carroll, Paul Nash, Petra Kopp,
Rebecca Furlong, Robbie Byrne, Rory O'Sullivan, Ruth Byrne, Shane
Golden, Erick Tran.

Printed in Great Britain
by Amazon